Dashing All the Way

S R SILCOX

JUGGERNAUT BOOKS

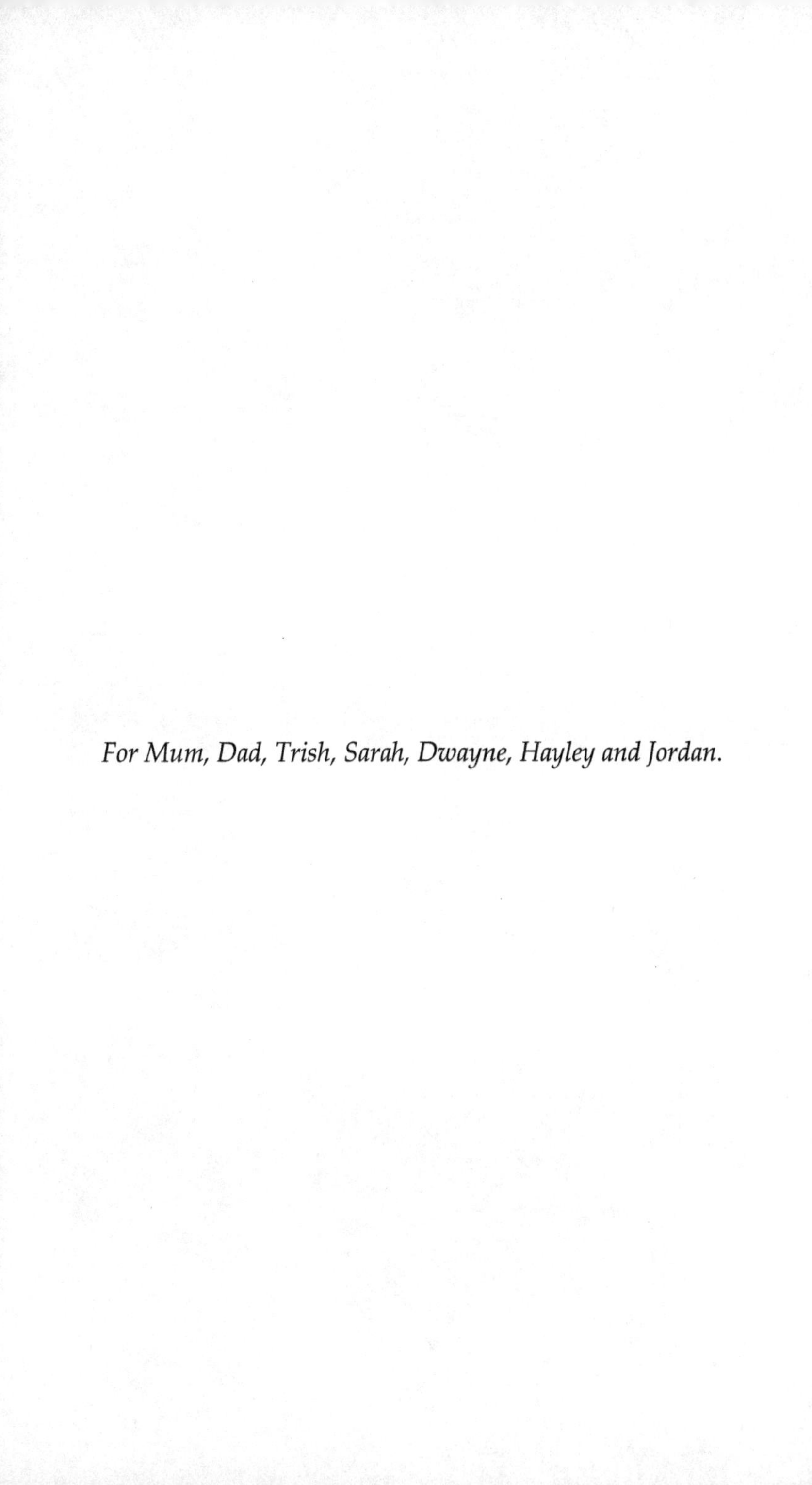

For Mum, Dad, Trish, Sarah, Dwayne, Hayley and Jordan.

Chapter 1

The air-conditioning was a nice reprieve from the heat building up outside and made the Christmas music in the jewellery store bearable. It wasn't that Mac didn't like Christmas. It just seemed to be starting earlier every year. Her boss had wanted to put up the tree in October this year, just so he could start the Christmas specials early to get people into the shop. Mac was glad she'd managed to talk him out of it. The first of November was her hard date on Christmas. Before then? She didn't want to think about the craziness that came with the Silly Season.

She leaned over the glass display case, looking at all the rings she could never afford. Even with their Christmas discounts, they were so far out of Mac's price range that she didn't want to even breathe on the glass. She listened as the man beside her decided between earrings and a necklace for his wife. So cliche,

Mac thought. Her girlfriend, Callie, wasn't into jewellery, which made it a little harder to buy her presents, but it was good for Mac's bank balance.

"Okay, Miss Mackenzie," the sales clerk said, handing Mac her receipt. "Just bring your receipt back in on Saturday to pick them up."

"Hooper," Mac replied.

"I beg your pardon?" the clerk asked, obviously confused.

"It's Mackenzie Hooper," Mac replied.

"Oh, I'm so sorry," the sales clerk said. She pulled the receipt back towards her, scribbled on the top and then handed it to Mac.

Mac shrugged. "Forget it. That's what happens when your parents give you a last name for a first name."

The sales clerk smiled, probably glad to not get yelled at for the mistake. Mac knew what that was like, dealing with the public at Christmas. No harm, no foul as far as she was concerned.

"I'll pick it up on Saturday then," Mac said, and as she turned to leave, her phone pinged in her pocket. She smiled when she saw it was a text from her friend, Sophie, reminding her to pick up the cheese platter from work for their dinner later. As she was texting Sophie back, she bumped into a couple coming into the store. When she lifted her head to apologise, her words got stuck in her mouth. Standing in front of her was her ex-girlfriend, Stacey.

"Oh! Mac!" Stacey said, plastering on one of those fake smiles she was famous for. "What are you doing here?"

"Hi, Stacey. Sorry. Gotta go," Mac replied, stepping to the side, trying not to make eye contact. Stacey could make a woman swoon just by looking at her and Mac wanted to avoid that at all costs.

But Stacey wasn't letting Mac go so easily. She turned to the woman with her and said, "This is my ex, Mac."

Mac did one of those awkward smiles and avoided the inevitable handshake by raising her hand in a wave.

"Oh, this is your—"

"—first love," Stacey finished with a laugh, but there was no humour in it.

Mac wanted to crawl into a hole and die, except for the fact that she had a girlfriend of her own at her house expecting her back any minute.

"But that was a long time ago, right, Mac?" Stacey continued, "Are you buying something for someone special?"

"Yes," Mac said a little too quickly. "Callie, my girlfriend."

Stacey smiled and nodded. "We're here to pick out rings ourselves, aren't we, Chase, sweetie."

"Oh, I'm not—" Mac started, but Stacey wasn't listening.

"It's wonderful to have someone who's just not afraid to tell the world they love you," Stacey continued.

"Literally," Chase said, making goo-goo eyes at Stacey. "I yelled my proposal from the top of Mt Coot-tha."

"And I yelled yes back," Stacey replied, giggling and making goo-goo eyes back.

The air had turned sickly sweet all of a sudden and Mac needed to leave before she threw up.

"Well, congratulations," Mac said, and she almost sounded like she meant it. "I have to get back to work, so I should let you get to it." She stepped to the side again, and this time Stacey brushed Mac's arm with her fingertips. Her touch sent shivers along Mac's skin, but not in a good way.

"Merry Christmas, Mac," Stacey said.

Mac pushed open the door and walked out into the heat outside. She took a long breath and let it out, ridding herself of the smell of the past, and headed to her car.

❧

Mac arrived home to find Callie in the back yard, raking up the leaves from the mango tree. She walked out onto the deck and leaned on a post. "Anyone would think you live here," she called smiling at her own joke. If everything went to plan over the next couple of weeks, that joke would become a reality.

Callie looked up, wiping her fringe from her forehead and smiling. "Hey, I wasn't expecting you home until later."

"Stanley let me finish on time today," Mac replied.

"That was nice of him," Callie said.

Mac could hear the sarcasm in her voice. Christmas was crazy busy at the shop and Stanley did not deal well with crazy or busy. "I think he's out of the doghouse with Maria," she said.

Callie scooped a pile of leaves into the green bin. "I hope it lasts. Because I want to spend some time with you before Christmas gets nuts."

"I know," Mac replied. Callie's shifts at the hospital ramped up heading in to Christmas, so every minute they got together this time of the year was a bonus. "I thought I'd take our presents to Soph and Kate to open tonight since we won't see them for Christmas."

"That's a good idea," Callie replied, dumping the last of the leaves in the bin. "Can you grab me some more clothes from my apartment while you're there?"

"Sure can," Mac said. "Just leave me a list and I'll get them on my way home."

A ball came sailing over the fence and landed almost at Callie's feet. She picked it up and threw it back.

"Thanks, Callie," a voice from over the fence called.

"You're welcome," Callie replied.

Mac shook her head. "I don't know why you do that. He'll never learn if you give them back."

Callie pulled a face. "I'm not getting in the middle of the feud you have with a twelve-year-old." She checked her watch. "I should go get ready for work. She handed Mac the rake and pecked her on the cheek as she walked up the steps. "Want to wash my back?"

Mac checked her watch. She had plenty of time before she had to be at Sophie's for dinner. She leaned the rake against the railing and hurried inside.

Chapter 2

Mac dropped down on the lounge beside her friend, Kate, who was wrestling a wad of tinsel. Sophie was setting out her snow globes on the table by the window. Sophie was a huge Christmas fan, and as per usual, her apartment was strewn with Christmas decorations, even though she wouldn't be home for Christmas this year. Mac had spent the best part of the last decade having Christmas together with her childhood friends, Sophie and Kate. This year was the first in a long time they wouldn't even be in the same city.

Sophie was flying out to Europe with her dad and Aunt Leila on Boxing Day after spending time with her dad's family in Melbourne. It would be the first time Aunt Leila had been back to the UK in over twenty years, and she wanted to celebrate her 70th birthday over there. Sophie was just excited to see snow and share her first ever white Christmas with her dad and aunt.

Kate had plans over Christmas, too, that she hadn't yet revealed, which made Mac wonder whether she'd gone back on her promise not to work over the holidays. Every year, Kate seemed to be working right up until the last minute on Christmas Eve and then be back at it straight after Boxing Day. Mac was convinced she'd work Christmas Day if they hadn't made plans with each other every year.

Even Mac would be away this year, travelling to Melbourne with Callie to spend Christmas with Callie's family. Although Mac's parents had visited once or twice, she'd never met Callie's parents. Callie hadn't been overly eager for Mac to meet them either, which was fine with Mac. She didn't like the meet-the-parents thing. She always seemed to get awkward around parents and say the wrong things. According to Callie, her family was busy running their party planning business anyway. This trip would be the first time Callie had been back to Melbourne in six years.

"How long since you've seen her?" Kate asked.

"Eight or nine years," Mac guessed.

"I thought Stacey had moved to Sydney?" Sophie asked, hanging a bauble on the tree, before pulling it off and hanging it in another spot.

"Typical," Mac said, taking the end of the tinsel Kate handed her and walked it over to Sophie. "She always seems to turn up when I'm happy."

Sophie swatted her. "She doesn't exist to make your life miserable."

"Could've fooled me," Mac said, helping Sophie wind the tinsel onto the tree.

"Enough about Stacey," Kate said. "I want to know what *you* were doing at the jeweller's?"

"Mac!" Sophie exclaimed, her mouth hanging open.

"I didn't say I was at the jewellers," Mac said, avoiding the question.

"I was having lunch at Cleo's and I saw you go in," Kate replied. "I would've come and said hi, but I was with someone."

"Ooh," Sophie said. "Who's the lucky guy?"

"We're not talking about me," Kate replied, a hint of red creeping into her cheeks.

"Oh, come on," Mac said. "Are you seeing someone?"

"Maybe," Kate said, a glint in her eye. "But Sophie and I want to know what you were doing at the jewellers."

"Getting a bit of bling for someone special?" Sophie asked, waggling her eyebrows.

"It's not what you think," Mac replied. She wasn't sure she wanted to tell them. When she'd first come up with the idea for Callie's present, she'd thought it was the best idea she'd ever had. Now that she was about to tell her friends, though, she was worried it was too cheesy.

"What is it then?" Kate asked.

"We need to know if you're making a life-changing decision," Sophie said.

"Why? So you can talk me out of it?" Mac asked.

"No, stupid. So we can help you plan it," Sophie replied.

Kate and Sophie both stared at Mac. Mac took a drink of her beer, hoping they'd get bored waiting if she didn't answer them. They didn't.

"Alright, alright. I'll tell you, but it's not what you think."

Sophie and Kate leaned forward in anticipation.

Mac repositioned an ornament on Sophie's tree. "I'm going to ask Callie—"

"—I knew it!" Sophie said. "Ooh, we're so excited, aren't we Kate?"

"It's not that exciting," Mac said.

"Of course it is. Our little Mackenzie, getting married," Kate said, grinning and rubbing Mac's hair into her head. "Who would have ever thought it?"

"Wait a minute," Mac said. "I'm not getting married."

"You aren't?" Sophie asked. There was a distinct air of disappointment in her voice. Mac had a feeling she'd already been thinking about the wedding decorations.

"No. I'm asking Callie to move in with me," Mac explained.

"Oh," Kate said, her shoulders drooping, just a little. "Well that's just as huge, isn't it Soph?"

"Of course it is," Sophie agreed. Although she was smiling, Mac could hear the disappointment in her voice. "Moving in is the first step before marriage."

"It's not the first step to anything," Mac said, shaking her head.

Kate laughed. "You do realise that you'd be living with Callie if you married her too, don't you?"

Mac swatted at her. "Of course I do. It's just…" She sighed. "Marriage is such a huge commitment. I'm not sure I'll ever be ready for that."

Sophie patted Mac's leg. "You're right. Marriage is a huge commitment and one I'm sure you'll give a lot of thought to once Callie's moved in."

Mac threw a pillow at her and Sophie and Kate both laughed. Then Kate put her hand on Mac's shoulder.

"We know how huge it is for you to ask Callie to move in with you after… Well, we won't go there."

"We're proud of you," Sophie said, cutting in.

Mac smiled. "Thanks."

"How are you going to ask her?" Kate asked.

"I got us matching keyrings engraved with our initials," Mac replied. "You know like those heart necklaces that break in half?"

Sophie and Kate looked at each other.

"What? Too cheesy?" Mac asked. "I knew it."

"Nope, not at all," Sophie assured her.

"Cute," Kate agreed.

"I'm not sure when I'll do it yet, though," Mac said. "I don't know if I want to ask her with her family on Christmas Day, or if I should ask her earlier."

"Wouldn't you want to ask her sooner rather than later? Asking her in front of her family might be too much pressure," Kate said.

"You don't want Callie to feel pressured to say yes," Sophie agreed.

"I did think of that. That's why I was thinking I might do it on the weekend. She's swapped rosters to have the night off. I'm thinking of taking her out somewhere nice and asking her then."

"Good idea," Sophie said. "Although asking her in public could be a problem too."

Mac sighed. "So I should just ask her at home? That's not very romantic."

"It would be if you made it a romantic night at home," Sophie suggested.

"Sophie's right," Kate agreed. "Why don't you get Maria to make up a nice picnic platter at work? That way you don't have to subject Callie to your cooking."

"Or make her cook herself," Sophie added.

Mac rolled her eyes. "I can cook."

"Barbecuing is not romantic," Sophie said.

"If I'd known you two were going to make it so complicated, I wouldn't have told you," Mac grumbled.

Kate patted Mac on the knee. "However you decide to do it will be fine. Right, Soph?"

"Right," Sophie agreed. "I'm sure everything will be fine." She stood up. "Anyone want another drink?"

"Not for me," Kate said. "I have to get going. I've got work in the morning."

"I thought you stopped working on weekends?" Mac asked.

"Yeah, well, I got lumped with a job that needs to be done before Christmas."

"Again? Kate…"

"I know, I know," Kate said, putting her hands up in defence. "I've negotiated overtime, so it's not that bad." She drained her wine glass and stood up. "I hope you have a really great time on your trip, Soph."

"Thanks," Sophie said, giving Kate a hug. "I'll send you lots of updates."

Mac stood up too. "I should get going as well. I have to grab some things from Callie's apartment."

"Ooh," Sophie said, pulling Mac in for a hug and jiggling her around excitedly. "I can't wait to hear how it goes tomorrow night."

Mac squeezed Sophie back. "Have a great time. And put up lots of photos so we can be jealous."

"I will," Sophie said. She waved to them as they left and closed the door behind them.

As Mac waited for the elevator with Kate, Kate said, "You know, it wouldn't surprise me if Callie asked you."

"What do you mean?"

Kate shrugged. "Just a feeling I get. I think she's ready to get married."

Mac chewed her lip. "I don't think I am."

"Well that's something you're going to have to think about, Mac. It's been almost a year. Don't you think you should start thinking about your future with Callie?"

"You sound like my mother," Mac said.

The elevator arrived and Kate stepped in.

"I'm just saying," Kate said. "Callie's a keeper. You'll really kick yourself if you lose her because you can't commit."

Mac nodded. "I know. That's why I'm asking her to move in with me."

Kate laughed. "It's a start, I guess." She waved as the doors closed, and Mac walked up the hallway to Callie's apartment. What if Kate was right and Mac had missed all of Callie's signals? She shook her head. They'd only been together a year. They both still had their own places, and the fact that Callie had been spending most of her time at Mac's was the reason she wanted her to move in. No. Despite what Kate had said, here was just no way Callie wanted to get married.

Chapter 3

Over the next few days, Mac had quietly plotted her plan of attack for her big moving in proposal. She'd tried to drop little hints in conversation, scoping out whether Callie would say yes to moving in, just to make sure. Confident that today was going to be the day, Mac rolled out of bed and pulled on a pair of shorts. She padded down the hallway and found Callie on her hands and knees, her head in the oven.

"Morning," Mac said.

"Morning," Callie replied. She sat up and smiled up at Mac. "Sorry. Was I being too noisy?"

"There's nothing sexier than lying in bed listening to the sounds of my girlfriend cleaning the house," Mac replied with a grin. She kissed Callie on the top of her head as she stepped past her to the bench.

Callie pulled off her gloves and tucked a stray blonde hair behind her ear. "That's not all that's sexy," she replied, standing up. She kissed Mac on the neck, giving her goosebumps. "But you're going to have to wait. I've got heaps more to do."

She took her bucket of cleaning supplies to the lounge room and started dusting the TV cabinet.

Mac popped a coffee pod into the top of the machine and turned it on. Her only plan this morning was to go out early to pick up Callie's present from the jeweller, and she had the perfect excuse. "I have to call in to see Stanley this morning. Something about the ordering for next week," she said over the gurgling of the coffee machine. It wasn't exactly a lie. She did need to go into work today, but not until this afternoon. It was the only thing that would get her out of the house without Callie thinking Mac was up to something. Any unusual moves Mac made around birthdays and Christmas made Callie suspicious.

Callie turned abruptly and said something back.

"What?" Mac couldn't hear Callie over the coffee machine.

Just as Mac turned the machine off, Callie yelled into the silence, "You can't go anywhere this morning."

"Why not?" Mac asked.

Callie hesitated. "I have a list of jobs I'd like you to do before you go anywhere."

"I won't be long," Mac said, sipping on her coffee. "An hour, maybe."

Callie sprayed Mr Sheen on the coffee table and rubbed furiously with a Chux. "You're never just an hour when you go into work."

Mac couldn't argue with that. She called into work quite a lot on short notice for Stanley to sort out some problem or other. And if she was going to use work as the reason to get out of the house to pick up Callie's present, she'd have to take at least the full hour so Callie wouldn't twig that something was up. Maybe she'd call in and see Kate at work too. It was on the way, and she'd said she'd be there today. "I'll do the jobs when I get back," Mac offered.

"I'd like you to do them before you go," Callie said. "Get them out of the way."

Mac checked her watch. It was 9.30am. The jeweller closed at 11.30am on Saturdays, and it'd take her about fifteen minutes to get there. And Mac needed to get there today because she was doing extra shifts at work leading up to Christmas to pay for their trip to Melbourne. Plus, she'd decided as of last night, thanks to Sophie's and Kate's advice, to ask Callie to move in tonight. A nice dinner at home, couple of drinks and then slip the box across the table. No pressure.

"Why do I have to do them this morning?" Mac asked.

"Because I'd like you to," Callie replied.

Mac thought about Callie's 'sexy' comment earlier. "Have you got something planned for this afternoon?"

"No," Callie replied without stopping her cleaning.

"Sure?" Mac pressed.

Callie stopped dusting and stood up, hands on hips. "I haven't got anything planned, I'd just like you to pull your weight."

Callie looked like she was as surprised by her outburst as Mac was. Mac decided not to argue.

"Where's the list?" she asked. She figured she could do a few jobs now, go out to pick up the present and then come back and do whatever was left.

Callie pointed to the dining table. Mac wandered over and looked at the list Callie had scrawled on the back of a real estate flyer. The usual things were on there: bathroom, toilet, unpack the dishwasher. But there were also other things Mac thought were unusual.

"Why do you want me to clean the barbecue and wash off the deck?" she asked.

Callie shrugged. "They haven't been done in a while."

"I'll do the barbecue before I use it next," Mac said. "And I'll do the deck this afternoon when it's cooler outside."

Callie crossed her arms. "Can you just do things when I ask you to for once?"

The sudden anger in Callie's voice made Mac start. And it made her wonder why Callie was so insistent that Mac do her jobs this morning before she went anywhere.

Callie had made a big thing about taking tonight off work but hadn't said why. They hadn't made any specific plans, but when Mac thought back on it now, every time she'd asked Callie what she'd like to do on her night off, Callie had been non-committal. Callie was rarely non-committal. Unless she was hiding something.

Mac thought back on her conversation with Kate last night and how she'd mentioned she thought Callie might be the one to pop the marriage question, not Mac.

Mac's stomach dropped. What if Callie was planning a romantic night at home so she could pop the question? Is that why she was so adamant about finishing the housework this morning? Callie was going to get in before Mac. Mac couldn't let that happen.

She took a gulp of her coffee and swallowed hard. What on earth was she going to do if Callie asked her? She needed to get out of the house, but she didn't want Callie to sense her panic.

"How about I do some of these jobs this morning, just an hour or so, and then I'll do the rest after lunch?" she offered. It would be cutting it fine, getting to the jeweller so close to closing, but she could make it if she cut through the back streets.

Callie looked at her watch. After some thought, she nodded. "Okay. An hour would be fine, but you can't hang around at work," she warned.

Mac smiled, relieved. "Fine. I'll do the inside stuff first and then the outside stuff after lunch." She drained her coffee, rinsed her mug and placed it on the sink. Then she got to work on Callie's list, keeping a careful eye on the clock.

❧

Mac was in the middle of cleaning the toilet when she heard it. The unmistakable sound of an RV driving down their street. She flushed the toilet, shoved the toilet brush in the stand and ripped off her gloves. She rushed out of the bathroom, down the hallway and flung open the front screen door.

Callie was standing on the grass, calling instructions to the driver as he backed the RV into their driveway. Beside her, also yelling instructions was Mac's mother.

"Mum?" Mac called.

Mac's mother turned, and grinned. "Surprise!" she said, throwing her hands into the air.

No wonder Callie had wanted to keep her at home this morning. She'd secretly invited Mac's parents for the weekend. Poor Callie. She had no idea what she'd done.

And then Mac had another thought. There was no way she'd be able to pick up Callie's present today. She'd have to figure out another way to pick it up, because there was no way she was leaving Callie alone with her parents.

Chapter 4

There was a knock on the door. "Mac? Are you in there? Your father needs to go."

Mac rolled her eyes. It was just like her father to need the toilet the minute someone else was in there.

"Who was that?" Kate asked.

"Mum," Mac replied. "Dad needs to go to the loo."

"Mac! I can't believe you'd call me when you're on the toilet."

"I'm not *on* the toilet, I'm *in* the toilet."

"I don't see the difference."

Mac huffed. "It's the only place I thought I wouldn't be disturbed."

Kate snorted.

"Look, Kate, can you help me or not?" Mac whispered furiously.

More knocking. "Mac?" It was Mac's father. "You need to hurry up or I'm going to—"

"—alright! I'll be out in a minute!" Mac called. To Kate she said, "Kate, please?"

Kate sighed. "Look, leave it with me. I'll see what I can do."

"Are you sure?"

"Yes, I'm sure. There's no way I'd want poor Callie to be left alone with your family until she gets to know them properly."

Mac let out a breath. "Thanks, Kate. I gotta go."

"That's gross, Mac," Kate said.

"Not like that," Mac replied. She hung up and put the phone in her pocket. Then she flushed the toilet, washed her hands, and splashed some water on her face.

When she opened the bathroom door, her father was leaning on the wall outside. When he saw his chance, he pushed past Mac and slammed the door shut without a word. Mac made a mental note to tell Callie to steer clear of the toilet for at least a couple of hours. As she headed back out to the lounge room, she wondered if she had enough beer in the fridge to cope with the weekend.

❧❦

Later, when Mac's dad was in the middle of a story about a road trip they'd done last year, the doorbell rang. Conversation stopped for a moment, with Callie glancing at Mac confused. "Surprise! Your family's here too," Mac joked.

Callie narrowed her eyes.

"I'm kidding. I'll get it," Mac said, hurrying to the door. She opened it a crack, saw the courier uniform and stepped outside, closing the door behind her.

"Andy," the courier said. "Friend of Kate's. You must be Macca."

"Mac," Mac corrected him. "Kate's never mentioned an Andy."

"Well, we're new friends. Sort of. I deliver stuff for the place where she works."

"Right," Mac said. "Did you pick up my package?"

"Yep. Got it right here." Andy thrust forward a small, gift-wrapped box.

The door opened behind them. Mac pulled the present into her, hiding it with her hands.

"Everything alright out here?" Mac's mum asked.

"Fine, Mum. I'll be in in a minute."

Mac's mum nodded and went back inside.

"What do I owe you?" Mac asked.

"Nothing. It was a favour for Kate. Besides, I'm off the clock."

"Are you sure?"

Andy shrugged. "You can shout me a beer next time we see each other."

Bad deal for him, since she was unlikely to see him again. "Deal," she agreed. "Thanks again."

"You're welcome," Andy replied, and turned and headed back to his van.

Callie and Mac's dad had moved out to the deck, so Mac took the opportunity to slip the present underneath the tree while Callie was distracted.

As she grabbed a beer from the fridge on her way past the kitchen, her mum appeared from the bedroom. "Do you need another drink, Mum?"

"I'd love a cup of tea, if that's okay. I've had enough wine for now."

"Sure," Mac replied, flicking the switch on the kettle. She pulled a mug down from the cupboard and set it on the bench. "I'll leave the tea and sugar out so you and Dad can help yourselves. You know where everything else is."

"Thanks, love," Mac's mum replied. She leaned back on the bench, her arms crossed, looking out the window to the deck. "Callie's a lovely girl."

"I know," Mac replied.

"Be a shame to mess this one up."

Mac dropped the spoon into the mug. "Mum..."

"I'm just saying. You waited too long last time and look where that got you."

"Can we not talk about it now?"

"I'm sorry, Mackenzie. I can just see the way she looks at you. And she obviously makes you happy."

"She does." Mac poured hot water into the mug, added milk and stirred. She handed the mug to her mum. "I won't mess it up."

Mac's mum took the mug and had a sip. "Your father and I just want you to be happy."

"I know," Mac replied. "I am." She picked up her beer and followed her mum outside where Callie was telling Mac's dad about their trip to Melbourne.

"Are you going to the Christmas carols down there? I hear it's a pretty big event," Mac's dad asked.

"Mac doesn't like crowds," Callie replied.

"And Callie's not into Christmas carols," Mac said. They both turned to look at Mac as she sat down.

"What?" Mac asked, taking a swig of her beer.

"Who was at the door?" Mac's dad asked.

"Oh. Pay TV guy," Mac lied.

"You didn't sign us up again, did you?"

Mac laughed. "Of course not." That was an argument she didn't want to have again. Besides, she'd been dropping hints for Callie that a pay TV sports package was high on her Christmas wish list.

"They're really sneaky those salesmen," Mac's mum said. "You have to be careful. You say one wrong thing and the next thing you know you're signed up for some holiday house group share scheme."

"That was one time twenty years ago," Mac's dad said. "And anyway, we got our money's worth before we pulled the pin. That house down on the Clarence was a nice place."

Mac's mum nodded, looking off into the distance. "It was, too. We should take the van back down that way one day."

Mac took a long drink of her beer as she listened to her parents go off on another travel story tangent, secretly hoping 'one day' would definitely be tomorrow.

Chapter 5

Later in the afternoon, and a few beers in, Mac was finally feeling more mellow about her parents' sudden appearance. It wasn't that she didn't want to see them. It was more a case of having to mentally prepare for their arrival. She needed time to adjust to having them in her house, because for two people, they seemed to take up a huge amount of space. And her father had a habit of sitting in Mac's recliner, meaning she was relegated to the soccer ball bean bag on the floor.

Mac was lounging on that bean bag, half-listening to her mum and Callie talking about scone recipes when her dad said, "We should do presents."

"Yes!" her Mum exclaimed. She clapped her hands like an overexcited child and moved from the dining table to the lounge room. "Did you bring them in?" she asked Mac's dad.

"They're in the bag by the tree," Mac's dad replied.

Mac's mum set about pulling presents out of a Santa sack beside the tree and passing them to Mac's dad.

"Can't we wait til after dinner?" Mac asked. She hadn't had the chance to go shopping for her parents yet so didn't have anything to give them. Waiting until after dinner meant she could use work as an excuse to go and get them something small.

"Now's okay," Callie said, smiling at Mac. She sat on the rug between Mac and the Christmas tree, curling her legs up underneath her.

Mac's dad passed a present each to Mac and Callie. Mac's mum said, "You have to open them together."

She looked so pleased with herself, Mac wondered whether she should be worried. Mac looked over at Callie who began to rip at the wrapping paper. Mac did the same until she had a pile of it on the floor in front of her, and a huge, fluffy blue towel on her lap.

"Open it out," Mac's dad said.

Mac and Callie unfolded the towels. Embroidered on Callie's towel was 'Hers', and on Mac's, 'Hers too'. Callie burst out laughing and Mac couldn't help but smile. The joint towel present was a sure sign her parents had accepted Callie into the family.

"Very clever," Callie said. "Thanks. Now I just have to talk Mac into replacing the rest of her old towels and sheets."

"What's wrong with my stuff?" Mac asked, slightly offended.

"Nothing," Callie assured her, patting her on the leg. "I'm joking."

"You open yours for each other now," Mac said to her parents.

"Not til they open ours," Callie said. She leaned across Mac and dug around under the tree. Mac's present for Callie tumbled out onto floor and Callie picked it up, curious. She looked at Mac and raised an eyebrow. Mac put her hand out to take it, but Callie placed it back under the tree and produced two other presents and handed them to Mac's parents.

Mac had no idea where they'd come from. Callie had obviously been shopping without her. She grabbed Callie's hand and gave it a squeeze. Callie turned and winked.

Mac's mum opened her present first, carefully picking apart the wrapping paper. She'd done that ever since Mac could remember. Anything she could save, she'd save. It drove her mad. Finally, the wrapping paper folded and placed on the floor beside her, she held up a new Kindle. "Oh, how wonderful!" she said, turning it over to read the back. "Barbara Kelly was talking about these just the other day, wasn't she Doug?"

"She was," Mac's dad confirmed.

"You were saying last time we spoke about how hard it was to take books with you when you went travelling," Callie said. "Mac and I thought this would be perfect for you."

Last time they spoke? How often did Callie and Mac's mum talk to each other?

"So, how do I read books on it?" Mac's mum asked, opening the box.

"We'll set you up with an account later and I'll show you how to download books," Callie said. "We'll probably have to charge it up first though."

Mac's mum beamed. "Thank you, girls."

"You're welcome," Mac said. "Your turn, Dad." Mac was curious to see what Callie had bought her father, someone who was notoriously hard to buy for.

Mac's dad carefully unwrapped the paper and passed it to Mac's mum, who folded it and placed it with her neatly folded wrapping. He turned the box over in his hands and then burst out laughing. "It's a fishing game!" he exclaimed. He opened the box and pulled the game controller out. "Look, love. It looks just like a fishing rod." He made a jiggling motion with it on his lap as if he were hauling in a fish.

"Now you don't have to worry about the weather," Callie said. "And it'll stop you from driving Sandra crazy when you're in the van."

Mac looked at Callie in awe. How on earth she could know her parents so well in only a year was amazing, considering she hadn't been able to work them out over the last thirty.

"Your turn girls," Mac's mum said.

"Oh, no, we don't have to open anymore," Mac said. "And you have to open each other's anyway."

Callie shrugged. "We can open one, can't we?"

Mac thought about the presents she had under the tree for Callie already. She still had a few more she had to buy before their trip to Melbourne, but there was one or two Callie could open today. She could give her the new keyboard cover for her tablet. She knew Callie would be excited about that. She'd been eyeing them off for ages.

Then again, she could give Callie the keyring. She thought about what Sophie and Kate had said about asking Callie to move in in public. She was sure Callie would say yes, anyway, and her parents weren't 'the public'. They were family. Besides, what better way for Mac to prove to both of her parents she was serious about Callie than to ask her to move in with her right now, in front of them? And she wasn't going to get the chance tonight anyway, so why not now?

"Sure. Why not?" Mac said.

Callie reached under the tree and passed a present to Mac. She waited expectantly for Mac to do the same. Mac picked up the smallest box under the tree and handed it to Callie. Callie raised an eyebrow and Mac just smiled.

"Open yours first," Callie said. "I have a feeling you want me to open this last."

Mac shrugged. "Okay." She ripped open her present to discover a brand new Cutters T20 away jersey. She held it up in front of her and grinned at Callie. "Thanks, babe. Just what I wanted."

"I know," Callie replied. She turned to Mac's parents. "She's only been dropping hints about it for the last six months."

Mac's parents laughed.

"Your turn," Mac said.

Callie carefully pulled at the ribbon, untied it and placed it on the floor beside her. Then she peeled back the wrapping paper, revealing a blue jeweller's box. She looked at Mac, cocking her head to the side. Mac swallowed, hoping Callie liked the split heart keyrings she'd had engraved with their initials. She'd have the one with Callie's initials on and Callie would have hers. She hoped Callie didn't think it was too cheesy.

As Callie lifted the lid on the box, Mac said, "Callie, will you m—"

Before Mac could get the question out, Callie launched herself at Mac, knocking her backwards.

"I thought you'd never ask," Callie said into Mac's ear.

"Really? So you will, then?"

Callie squeezed Mac harder. "Of course I will." Mac grinned and looked at her parents. Mac's mum had her hand on her chest and her dad's eyes were wide. Mac was secretly pleased at how excited they were at Callie agreeing to move in with her. They'd seen Mac endure so many false starts with relationships over the years, they were obviously genuinely happy for her to finally have found someone like Callie. And if she was totally honest, it was good seeing her parents' reactions after all the pressure they'd put on her about not stuffing up with Callie.

Then Callie sat back down, opened the box, pulled out a ring and placed it on her ring finger. Mac watched, numb, as Callie gushed over the ring with her parents, while she tried desperately not to throw up.

Chapter 6

Mac locked herself in the bathroom for a second time that day, furiously leaving whispered messages for Kate to call her back. Sophie also hadn't answered her phone, but Mac wasn't really expecting her to. She would've been knee deep in packing for her UK trip.

She'd also called the jeweller who, as she already knew, was closed for the day and helpfully reminded her there was just two more weeks before Christmas. She was hoping for an emergency after hours number, like doctors and vets had, but there was no way for her to tell them about her ring emergency.

Mac tried Kate one last time, but she got the voice mail again and decided to try her again tomorrow after her parents had left. She flushed the toilet, so Callie and her parents didn't think she was avoiding them — again — and went back outside.

Callie and Mac's mum were already discussing possible venues and the way Callie kept touching the ring made Mac's stomach churn. Mac's dad offered her a beer, and she accepted gratefully. He pulled her outside to the deck and patted her on the back. "You should've told your mother and me," he said.

Mac took a long drink of her beer. "Why?"

"Because your mother wanted you to have your grandmother's ring for when you got married."

"I didn't know that," Mac said, which was the truth.

"Well now you do. That ring's supposed to be handed down to whoever gets married first, and let's be honest. It's not like Bryce is going to get married any time soon."

Mac's older brother had been with his girlfriend for close to six years now. He had no intention of getting married and neither did his girlfriend, as far as Mac could tell.

"It's not really my style though, that ring," Mac said.

"It's not for you," Mac's dad said. "You could've given it to Callie."

"Maybe I could give it to her for our anniversary," Mac suggested, though why she said it, she didn't know. It wasn't like they were going to have an anniversary since they weren't actually going to get married.

"Maybe," Mac's dad said. "Anyway, I'm proud of you. Your mother is too."

"Thanks, Dad." It was the first time in a long time she'd heard her dad say that. Mac tried not to focus on how disappointed her parents were going to be when they found out it was all a big mistake.

A ball came sailing over the fence into the back yard. "What was that?" Mac's dad asked.

"Kid next door," Mac replied, walking out onto the grass and picking up the ball. "Another one you're not getting back," she called over the fence.

"Get stuffed," came the reply.

Mac walked back onto the deck and dropped the ball into a bucket on top of the others that her twelve-year-old neighbour had sent over the fence in the last year.

"Just throw it back," Mac's dad said.

"He won't learn to not hit them over if I keep throwing them back."

"Looks like it's working," Mac's dad said, indicating the bucket with his beer bottle and smiling at Mac.

A ball hit the fence, and then another one, followed by another one. "Bloody Justin," Mac muttered under her breath. "See what he does? This is why I don't give the balls back."

Mac's dad clapped her on the shoulder. "Let's head inside and save your new fiancé from your mother. She's probably started on the guest list by now."

Mac's stomach churned again as she followed her dad inside. She had to think of a way out of this situation, and fast, before any more damage was done.

Later that night as Mac lay in bed listening to her father's snores from the spare room, she finally had time to herself to think. She slid out of bed and tiptoed down the hallway to the kitchen. She poured herself a glass of cold water and slipped quietly through the back door to the deck where she sat down on the back step and leaned against a post.

The afternoon had been filled with Callie and Mac's mum discussing options for their wedding, and Mac tried hard to not get involved. Whenever she was asked her opinion, Mac had replied either "I haven't really thought about it yet" or "Whatever Callie thinks." She figured the less involved she seemed to be now, the easier it would be to tell Callie the truth.

Mac heard the screen door slide open and turned to see Callie standing in the doorway, her blonde hair askew, her pyjama top hanging down exposing a shoulder.

"Everything okay?" she asked.

"Yeah. Just can't get to sleep."

"Big day," Callie said, sitting down beside Mac on the step. She lay her head on Mac's shoulder.

Mac kissed the top of Callie's head and wrapped an arm around her waist. "A bit,' she replied.

"Sorry if it was too much," Callie said. "Your mum and I wanted to surprise you."

"That's okay," Mac replied. At least that was the truth. Her parents arriving out of the blue was the least of her worries.

"Your mum said it was really hard to surprise you," Callie said. "I told her I accepted the challenge."

Mac laughed. "So it's my fault?"

"Exactly," Callie replied. "You know how much I like a challenge." She sat up and smiled at Mac.

It melted Mac's heart.

"And the wedding stuff, I didn't mean to go all crazy about it," Callie said. "We haven't even set a date yet."

Mac shrugged. "Don't worry about it."

Callie lay her head back down on Mac's shoulder. "It's quiet out here at night."

"Because Justin's in bed asleep," Mac replied.

Callie let out a chuckle.

They sat in silence for what seemed like ages, Mac sipping on her water, Callie tucked in beside her. Mac considered telling Callie the truth, since it was just the two of them, but it was just too perfect a moment to destroy.

Mac's dad's snoring was just barely audible, and when he snorted a loud one, Mac and Callie both giggled.

"I love you, you know," Callie said all of a sudden.

"I know," Mac replied. Callie flicked her on the leg. "Ow! Okay, I love you too."

Callie kissed Mac on the cheek. "I'm going to bed before your dad starts snoring again. Don't be too long."

"I won't," Mac replied. She watched as Callie slipped back inside and then looked out over the back yard. How on earth was she going to tell Callie the truth without ripping her heart out?

Chapter 7

The next morning, Mac felt surprisingly good, considering the mess she found herself in. She promised herself that as soon as her parents had left, she'd sit Callie down and tell her the truth. It was like ripping off a band-aid. She felt so good, in fact, that she cooked a barbecue breakfast for Callie and her parents, while Callie set Mac's mum up with a new email address and loaded up her kindle with books. It turned out that Mac's dad had bought her mum a hundred-dollar gift card for Amazon, which is why the kindle had to be opened before her dad's present yesterday.

Mac's mum wasn't much for technology, and although her dad could at least work out the DVD player in the RV, they were yet to work out how to use video calling on their mobile phones. Texting was a stretch, but her mum could manage it at a pinch, although her random capitalisation sometimes made Mac laugh.

Mac marvelled at Callie's patience as she listened to her re-explain for the third time how the books were digital files and not photos of the paper books, and how they magically appeared on the kindle. If it had been left to Mac to sort out her mother's new kindle, it would have ended in an argument and most likely a tantrum (Mac's) within the first five minutes.

Callie was telling Mac's mum all about the virtues of Facebook for keeping up with friends and family when Kate called. Mac passed the barbecue tongs to her dad to take the call.

"Mac! I'm so sorry I didn't call back last night. What happened?"

"I actually can't talk right now, Kate. Can I call you back?"

"Oh. Everyone's still there?"

"Who's that?" Mac's mum asked.

"Kate," Mac replied.

"Oh! Say hi from me," Mac's mum said.

"Mum says hi," Mac said.

"Say hi back," Kate said.

Mac relayed the message and her mum smiled.

"Sounds like you're busy. I'll call you back later," Kate said.

"I can call you," Mac replied.

"It's okay," Kate said. "Hang on." There were some muffled voices in the background and a sound Mac couldn't quite place. "Sorry, Mac. It's probably easier if I call you. Actually, are you at work this afternoon?"

"I have to go in at one."

"What time do you finish?"

"Six. Why?"

"Can I call in and see you at work?"

"I guess so."

"Seven?" Kate asked.

"Six," Mac replied.

"No, sorry I wasn't talking to you, Mac. I'll see you this afternoon."

"Okay," Mac replied. She hung up feeling confused. Who on earth was Kate talking to?

❧

Mac's parents left mid-morning, heading south for the rest of the summer. Mac's mum was loaded up with ebooks for the trip and Mac's dad was well-practised on his new fishing game. Callie and Mac had both had a turn on it before her dad packed it away. Callie boasted for nearly an hour about the size of her virtual fish compared to Mac's. Mac's dad assured Callie he'd keep her updated on how well he was doing. It was all surreal really. Mac had never known her parents to take to any of her girlfriends like they had to Callie. Then she remembered that as far as they knew, Callie was going to be their daughter-in-law, and her heart sank. She was definitely going to have to tell Callie today.

As they waved Mac's parents off, Callie said, "I've been called in to work. Rosie's called in sick."

"No. Really? I thought we had a few more hours together," Mac said.

"Sorry. I managed to put off my start time to see your parents this morning, but I have to go in now."

"What time are you finishing?" Mac asked.

"Eight, I think."

"That's late."

Callie wrapped Mac in a hug. "I know. But the flip-side is that I don't have to go in tonight." She kissed Mac on the lips and then whispered, "Let's do something romantic."

Mac grinned. "Okay."

Callie pulled away. "I have to get ready."

Mac followed Callie back inside. At least she'd have a bit more time to come up with how she was going to tell Callie the truth. And she'd get to ask Kate's advice before she did it. At least that was a bonus of Callie getting called into work.

Her phone buzzed in her pocket. It was a text from her mother. *'Thanks for having Us love. Very Happy for you and Callie. Dad said He'll Find grandma's ring and Bring it Next Time. Love to you Both xx'*

Chapter 8

At work that afternoon, Mac was so distracted by the Callie situation that she unpacked four boxes of Pink Lady apples onto the Red Delicious display before she realised. She decided after she'd repacked them, she should probably spend the day out the back of the shop instead. Stanley wouldn't be happy for customers to walk out of the shop with the more expensive apples at a much cheaper price.

She was ticking off deliveries on a clipboard when there was a tap on her shoulder. Mac spun around to see Kate standing there.

"Hey," Kate said, pulling Mac into a hug.

"Hey yourself," Mac said, hugging Kate back.

"I'm so sorry I didn't call you back," Kate said. "Tell me what happened."

Out of the corner of her eye, she saw that courier guy, Andy, walk in. "Just wait a sec. I think I have to go take a delivery."

Kate turned to see where Mac was looking. "Oh, no, Andy's with me."

"What do you mean?"

Kate shrugged. "We're sort of dating," she said with a lop-sided grin.

Mac's jaw dropped open.

Kate rolled her eyes. "Don't look so surprised."

"It's just... you? And him?" Mac could barely put full sentences together. Kate had resisted dating for as long as Mac could remember. Her career had come first, above even time spent with Mac and Sophie sometimes.

Mac tried to process this information as she glanced over to Andy, who was talking to Maria about picnic platters. She looked back to Kate and it dawned on her what Kate was trying to tell her. "Kate! You have a boyfriend!"

"Shh," Kate said, pulling Mac away. "He's not my boyfriend. At least, I don't think so." She looked back at him. "We haven't discussed it yet."

"But you're seeing him?"

"I guess so."

Mac grinned. "Look at you getting down and dirty with the courier guy."

Kate punched Mac on the shoulder. "Shut up."

"How long for?" Mac asked.

Kate shrugged. "A couple of weeks."

"A couple of weeks? Why didn't you say anything?"

"I didn't know where it was going. I didn't want to get you and Sophie excited about something that might not work out."

Mac nodded. She recalled how excited Sophie and Kate were when Mac and Callie had made their relationship official. They'd both married Mac and Callie off within the first couple of months. That thought made her remember why she needed to talk to Kate.

"Speaking of not working out," Mac said. "I need your advice."

"Oh, yes! Sorry. I didn't come here to go on about Andy. So, tell me, what's going on with Callie?"

Mac sighed. "I accidentally asked her to marry me."

"You what?" Kate's mouth dropped open. "That's great, Mac. But I thought—"

"Don't get too excited," Mac replied. "I didn't mean to."

"What happened?"

"Your courier guy picked up the wrong present," Mac said. "He picked up a ring instead of my keyring."

Kate's hand flew to her mouth. "He wouldn't do that," she said.

"Well he did. And now Callie and my parents think we're getting married."

Kate started laughing. "I'm so sorry, Mac. I know it's not really funny."

"Then stop laughing," Mac said.

Kate took a breath and pulled herself together. "Sorry. What are you going to do?"

"I have no idea. That's why I wanted to talk to you. I need help."

"That's a given," Kate replied. She giggled again. "Sorry."

Mac punched Kate on the arm. "This is serious, Kate. It's not my ring. It's someone else's and we've probably stuffed up someone else's proposal by the looks of the diamond in it."

"Well, that is a problem," Kate agreed. "Why haven't you told her yet?"

"I tried," Mac replied. "But she got called in to work so I didn't get a chance to."

"You have to tell her, Mac," Kate said. "If you really don't want to be engaged, you can't keep stringing her along."

Mac sucked in a breath and let it out. "I know. I just don't know how to tell her."

"How about the truth?" Kate suggested. "If Andy did pick up the wrong present like you say he did, then it's not your fault. I'm sure Callie will see that."

"Maybe," Mac said.

Kate grabbed Mac by the shoulders. "Callie loves you, Mac. You're both going to look back on this and laugh about it."

Mac wasn't so sure. She knew Kate was right, though. The sooner she ripped off the band-aid, the better it would be for everyone. She caught sight of

Stanley out of the corner of her eye. He tapped his watch.

"I have to go. Stanley's riding my backside today. I think he's fighting with Maria again."

Kate looked over to where Andy was still talking to Maria. He looked up and gave them a wave. Kate waved back. "You'll be fine," she said to Mac.

"I hope so," Mac replied.

Kate pulled Mac into a hug. "Call if you need me."

"I will. And congratulations," Mac replied, nodding towards Andy.

Kate glanced across to Andy and smiled. "Thanks."

Mac watched as Kate walked over to Andy and looped her hand through Andy's arm. They waved as they left, and though Mac smiled and waved back, she had a distinct feeling of dread in the pit of her stomach. She hoped Kate was right about Callie and how she'd react. The one thing Mac swore she'd never do is disappoint her, and here she was, about to blow that promise clean out of the water.

Chapter 9

When Mac heard Callie's car in the driveway, she lit the candles on the table. Although Callie would have had dinner at work, Mac had brought home some of Maria's Tiramisu for dessert. She figured it might get Callie on side for the disappointment that was about to come.

Mac strode to the door and opened it, just as Callie started up the front steps. She stopped mid-stride and looked up. She wasn't smiling.

"We need to talk," she said, continuing up the steps and pushing past Mac in the doorway. Mac's stomach dropped. Somehow, Callie must know. Mac decided to let Callie make the first move.

Callie tossed her keys on the table by the door and dropped her bag on the floor beside it. She pulled off her shoes and dropped down onto the lounge.

"I've got Tiramisu," Mac offered, heading to the dining table. "Want some?"

Callie nodded tiredly. Mac dished out two serves of dessert and brought them to the lounge room. Mac knew she was stalling for time, but she needed to. She knew this conversation was not going to end well.

Callie took a mouthful of dessert and then said, "We agreed we wouldn't tell anyone about our engagement until I got the chance to tell my family."

Mac let out a breath she didn't know she'd been holding. It wasn't what she'd been expecting. It may just be worse. "What do you mean?"

"I got a call from Mum tonight while I was on break, asking why I hadn't had the decency to tell her and Dad myself about us getting engaged."

This was not good news. Now Mac would have to tell both sets of parents their engagement was a mistake. And she hadn't even met Callie's parents yet. She hoped it wouldn't mess with their holiday plans. "How did they find out?" Mac asked.

Callie lifted an eyebrow. "How do you think they found out?"

Mac shrugged. "I don't know. I didn't tell them."

"Your mother," Callie replied, as if the answer was plainly obvious.

"My mother told your mother?" Mac asked. "They don't even know each other."

"They didn't," Callie said. "Not until your mother plastered the news all over Facebook."

Mac snorted. "Mum's not on Facebook."

"Want a bet?" Callie asked.

Mac pulled her phone from her pocket and opened Facebook. Sure enough, there was a friend request from her mother. Mac accepted the friend request and then checked her mum's profile. She now had four friends. Bryce, Mac, Callie and Barbara Kelly. And sure enough, there on Callie's wall was a post welcoming her to the family. "Oh," was all Mac could manage.

"Oh, all right," Callie said. "My whole damn family's seen it now thanks to your mum. I mean, look how many comments and likes and hearts it's gotten."

"Oh, that's bad," Mac said. This was extremely bad, though not in the way Callie was apparently thinking.

Mac scrolled through the congratulations messages from Callie's friends and family on her mum's post. This was getting way out of hand. She had to do something about it.

"Callie, I—"

"It's okay. I know it's not your fault." Callie took the phone off Mac and placed it on the coffee table. Then she took Mac's hands in hers. "I know this is a huge thing for us. For you, even. And I have to be honest, a proposal was the last thing I was expecting."

"Me too," Mac said. At least that was the truth.

Callie smiled. "I'm glad you asked, though."

"You are?" Mac asked. This wasn't how the conversation was meant to be going.

"Don't get me wrong, I'm not happy I didn't get to tell Mum and Dad about it first, but," she shrugged. "At least they've sort of met your mum now."

"I guess," Mac replied.

Callie yawned. "I'm sorry. I'm pooped. I need to get to bed. I've got an early start tomorrow." She stood up and stretched.

"Callie, wait," Mac said.

"Yeah?"

Mac swallowed. It was now or never. "Do you want the rest of your dessert?"

Callie shook her head. "You can have it." She leaned down and kissed Mac on the lips. "Night, babe."

"Night," Mac replied.

As soon as Callie had disappeared into the bedroom, Mac picked up her phone and text Kate. *'Did not go to plan. Still engaged.'*

Kate replied with one word. *'Chicken'.*

Chapter 10

The next morning on her way to work, Mac called in to the jeweller to try to sort out the mistake. She still didn't know how she was going to tell Callie, but at least if she could get the real present, it might soften the blow. When she got to the shop, she was greeted with a closed sign. *'Closed for personal reasons. Will reopen Thursday 9am. Sorry for the inconvenience.'*

Mac sighed. She was working full days for the next week. She'd have to figure out a way to get an hour or two off to get to the shop on the weekend. She was fast running out of time. Callie was working night shifts until the end of the week, so they'd hardly see each other for the next few days. At least she had a few more days to come up with the plan of attack that had so far managed to elude her.

Sophie and Kate had been no help whatsoever either. Mac had spoken to each of them on the phone that morning, relaying the worst bits of her conversation with Callie last night. Sophie had at least been a little sympathetic especially since it was the first time she was hearing about it, but she had no ideas to help Mac out. She was distracted by her impending overseas trip and Mac couldn't blame her. No. Mac had no-one to blame for this situation but herself.

Kate sounded far too busy with Andy to be paying much attention to Mac and her problems. Mac was a little miffed that neither of her friends were taking it as seriously as they should. Then again, why should they? They weren't exactly unhappy that Mac was engaged to Callie, even if it was all a big fat lie.

Mac got in her car and drove to work, hoping that being busy might keep her mind off her stupid situation.

ತಿೀ⁊

The next two days were agony for Mac. She worked full days at the green grocers, leaving for work while Callie was still in bed, while Callie returned home from work in the early hours of the morning when Mac was asleep. Their only mode of communication was by notes left on the kitchen table. Callie had begun signing off on her notes with 'love, your fiancé', which made Mac's stomach twist into knots every time she read it.

To make matters worse, Sophie had flown to Melbourne with Leila and her dad for the first leg of their holiday and Kate had been so busy with Andy that Mac hadn't been able to nail her down for a catch up. Mac was starting to feel desperate, but at least she was going to be able to get to the jeweller's in two days to finally find out what had happened.

That afternoon, Mac got home to find Callie's car was still in the driveway. She immediately went into defence mode. Callie hardly ever missed a shift at work. She tentatively opened the front door, unsure about what she'd find inside, and was relieved to find Callie sitting on the lounge, apparently happy to see her.

"Everything okay?" Mac asked. "I thought you'd be at work."

"I'm okay," Callie replied. "I'm just starting a bit later tonight. I wanted to see your face when you opened your present."

Mac dropped her keys on the side table and walked over and sat down beside Callie on the lounge. "What present?"

"This one," Callie replied, handing Mac an envelope. "Mum and Dad sent through some early ones. I know what yours is already." She grinned. "Hurry up and open it."

"Okay," Mac said. She pried open the envelope and pulled out a card. Inside it said in neat, flowing handwriting *'Welcome to the family, Mackenzie'*. Inside the card were two tickets to the Boxing Day Test Match, and a Melbourne Cricket Club membership nomination form. Mac was aware that Callie was waiting for a reaction. She swallowed hard. The cricket tickets and the MCC membership were things she'd coveted for a long, long time. They were things she'd joked with Sophie and Kate about getting 'when she got rich'. They were things she'd never think she'd get. And now she'd finally gotten her hands on them. From her girlfriend's, - no, fiancé's - family. This was bad. Very, very bad.

Mac plastered on a smile. She hoped Callie couldn't see through it to the panic that was rising up in her stomach. She swallowed hard and couldn't seem to get enough air. The world started to spin, and her vision started to grey at the edges. The last thing she remembered before she blacked out was Callie asking if she liked her present.

Chapter 11

"You haven't even met Dad yet and you're already panicking about it," Callie joked as she checked Mac's medical chart.

Mac knew it was a joke, but she didn't find it funny. In fact, the whole situation had gotten out of hand so fast, Mac's head was spinning. Spinning so fast, in fact, she'd apparently had a panic attack.

"Nothing wrong with your heart," Callie said. "I could've told them that." She looked up at Mac and winked. Mac smiled weakly. Callie said, "They want to keep you in for observation. You should be able to come home when I finish my shift in the morning."

Mac's stomach grumbled. "Have I missed dinner?"

"I can organise something from the kitchen if you're hungry," Callie replied. "Might be an hour or so." She looked at her watch. "Actually, I'll grab something and come back on my break. We can have dinner together."

Mac nodded. "Okay."

There was a knock on the door and Mac turned to see Kate poke her head in. "Okay if I come in?"

"Sure," Callie replied. She turned to Mac. "I better get going." She kissed Mac on the forehead. "I'll see you in an hour or so with some dinner. Love you."

"Love you too," Mac replied.

"No excitement, Kate," Callie said as she left the room.

"No problem," Kate replied, pulling a chair over to the hospital bed and dropping down into it.

As soon as Callie left, Kate whispered, "You haven't told her yet, have you?"

Mac rolled her eyes. "I'm sort of busy at the moment, if you hadn't noticed."

"You've had the best part of a week, Mac. What happened?"

Mac sat up in her bed. "I just couldn't find the right time," she said.

"There's never going to be a right time," Kate said. "Is that how you ended up in here?"

"I got cricket tickets and a membership application for the Melbourne Cricket Club from Callie's family."

"I don't follow," Kate replied. "How did they make you have a panic attack?"

"Don't you see, Kate? I can't tell Callie now. The whole world knows thanks to my bloody mother being unable to work out how to send a private message on

Facebook. And then Callie's dad welcomes me into the family with cricket tickets? And an MCC membership? I'll never get that chance again!"

"You're putting cricket tickets over telling the truth?" Kate shook her head.

"No, but—"

"No buts, Mac. This is your own fault," Kate said. "You should've told her straight away."

"It's Andy's fault for picking up the wrong present," Mac replied.

"Leave Andy out of this," Kate said. "He just did what he was asked."

"If he'd checked the package—"

Kate held up her hand. "I'm not going to listen to you blame Andy for this. This mess is yours, Mac, and you need to deal with it, one way or another."

"What do you mean, one way or another? What other way is there?"

"Maybe you should think long and hard about what you really want, Mac," Kate said, her voice low.

"I am," Mac replied.

"Because she's nothing like Stacey," Kate continued. "You can't keep punishing your girlfriends because of one bad relationship."

"I'm not—" Mac started, but Kate was on a roll now. She paced across the room, glanced out of the window and turned back to Mac.

"Why do you always want to sabotage your own happiness?" Kate asked, throwing her hands in the air for emphasis. "Callie loves you."

"I know."

"And I know you love her," Kate said. She took a breath. "Look, Mac. I'm telling you this as one of your longest and best friends. That woman out there is worth fighting for."

Mac let out a long breath. "I know."

"And you have to work this out sooner, rather than later," Kate said.

"I know," Mac said.

"Know what?" Callie asked, poking her head around the door.

Mac jumped. How much had she heard? "How hungry I am," she lied.

Callie smiled. "The canteen's going to send up some sandwiches. I have some patients I have to check in on, but I'll be back in fifteen minutes or so."

"Okay," Mac said.

Mac and Kate both watched Callie leave.

"I really think," Kate whispered as she moved to the doorway. "That Callie might be a lot more understanding than you give her credit for. Do you really want to risk losing her over a stupid mistake?"

Mac sucked in a breath and let it out slowly. "No. I don't."

"Then I suggest you give it some thought," Kate said. "I'll call you tomorrow, see how you are. Okay?"

"Okay."

Kate walked toward the door.

"Kate?"

Kate turned. "Yeah?"

"Thanks."

"What for?"

"For being the logical one."

Kate smiled. "You're welcome."

Mac thought about Kate's advice long after she left. She was right. In the grand scheme of things, Mac really didn't want to lose Callie. She wanted to live with Callie, make a life with Callie. Would getting married really be so bad?

Chapter 12

At home the next morning, Callie climbed into bed and snuggled in beside Mac. "Feeling okay?" she asked.

"I'm good," Mac replied.

Callie took Mac's hand and entwined their fingers. "You gave me a fright last night. You know that?"

"Sorry."

"I didn't realise how much this whole engagement thing was affecting you."

"It's not that bad," Mac replied.

"It's a big thing, getting married," Callie continued.

"I know," Mac replied.

"And we don't have to rush anything," Callie said. "We'll wait until after Christmas to talk about a date and all the other stuff."

In reply, Mac kissed the top of Callie's head and breathed in the fresh scent of shampoo. Callie had popped in every hour last night at the hospital, checking on her and sitting with her. Mac had woken early that morning to find Callie asleep on a chair in the corner, a rug pulled up around her shoulders. As Mac had watched Callie sleeping, her head leaned back on the chair and her mouth ajar, she'd begun to realise that Kate had been right.

Mac had never been happier than she had been over the last twelve months. The house had never felt more like a home than when Callie was pottering around inside while Mac was on the deck or working in the yard.

And waking up with Callie snuggled into her every morning or climbing quietly into bed after a night shift was something Mac had gotten used to the last few months.

And then there was Mac's family. Callie had fitted in so easily, which was no mean feat. Mac found her family a handful sometimes, but Callie obviously loved being around them and having them around. She even got her dad's weird sense of humour.

Mac ran her fingers through Callie's damp hair and in response, Callie looked up. "What?"

Mac smiled. "Nothing. Just...I love you."

Callie grinned. "Aw, I love to you too."

Mac pulled her arms tighter as Callie snuggled her head back onto Mac's chest.

Nope. There was no way Mac was going to lose her to a stupid mistake. She knew she couldn't afford the ring Callie currently had. She'd checked the jeweller's online store on her phone earlier and almost had another panic attack at the price. The only thing she could afford was the keyrings she'd already bought. As much as she didn't want to, she'd have to ask her dad for her grandmother's ring and hope it was enough.

She'd have to tell Callie about the ring mistake, of course, but she'd just say that they got mixed up, and that even though it wasn't the right ring, it was the intent behind it. She just had to work out a way to get the wrong one off of Callie's finger and back to the jeweller to give to the rightful owner.

Mac brushed the engagement ring with her thumb and felt it move. It gave her an idea. "It's a bit big," she said.

Callie pulled her hand away and twisted the ring on her finger. "A bit. I'll need to get it resized."

"I can do it," Mac said, a little too quickly. "I mean, it'll be easier for me to get to the jeweller. It's close to work."

"Are you sure?"

"I'm sure. Just tell me what size and I'll tell the jeweller."

Callie smiled. "It'll be nice to have it fitting properly when we go to Melbourne. No chance of it falling off." She squeezed Mac in a hug and Mac hugged her back. Mac felt lighter than she had done in weeks.

Chapter 13

Deciding to actually go through with the engagement had taken a load off Mac's mind and she felt happier than she had in ages. She'd dropped the ring back to the jeweller's, who was eternally grateful to have it back, and picked up the key rings. She told Callie the jeweller would call when the ring was ready, hoping that would buy her some time to get the replacement couriered from her parent's place. She was also thinking of asking Callie properly, since it hadn't really gone to plan the first time. As for the key rings, Mac had decided to add them to Callie's stocking, as a fun gift to make it official that Callie moved into the house.

The day before she was due to go back to work, she was lounging in the hammock on the deck, thinking of ways to pop the question officially when she heard the unmistakable crash of ball on fence. In between the intermittent banging came mumbling and what surprised Mac was that it was the middle of the day. Justin should have been at school.

Mac was determined to not let Justin ruin her mood, or her attempts to have a nap, so she climbed out of the hammock, and stuck her head over the fence. Justin stood a few metres away and pelted a ball that hit a spot just above a scrubby looking plant that had obviously seen better days before Justin had come along.

Justin trudged over and picked up the ball and as he stood back up, he noticed Mac peering over the fence. "What do you want?" he asked.

"Why aren't you at school?" Mac countered.

"Got suspended," Justin replied, flinging the ball at the same spot on the fence. He had a good radar, Mac thought. And a good arm. She wondered if he played cricket on the weekends.

"What for?" Mac asked.

"What do you care?" came the defiant reply.

"Because I'm supposed to be resting after I got out of hospital, not that you care, and you're making it bloody hard to do that with all your banging."

"So?"

"So?" Mac said. "So? Stop bloody banging or I'll tell your parents."

Justin snorted. "Good luck with that." He let another ball loose, hitting the exact same spot.

"They're not home?" Mac asked.

"Nup."

Another ball hit the same spot. He had a really good aim. Too good to be putting balls over the fence as often as he did. That made her just a little curious. Mac thought about what her dad had said about talking to him, and she was probably going to regret it, but she asked, "Why'd you get suspended?"

"I hit Maisy Walker in the head with a dodge ball in PE," Justin replied.

"On purpose?" Mac asked, surprised you could get suspended for something like that.

"Yep," Justin replied. He threw another ball and hit the fence.

"Why would you do that?"

Justin didn't answer. Instead, he threw another ball but threw wide. His shoulders drooped and he trudged over and picked up the ball and walked back to his mark. He threw again, this time getting closer but not hitting the target.

Mac thought about why a boy would deliberately hit a girl in the head with a ball. There could be only one of two reasons. Either she was a bully and he used PE as his chance to get her back, which was probably unlikely. Or he liked her. Mac knew from experience with her older brother that boys Justin's age could do some stupid things around girls they liked. Bryce, for example, once jumped off the shed into a wading pool filled with water to impress a girl. He impressed her all right, with two broken legs, and being in traction for a month. She did visit him in hospital, so there was that.

"You like her, don't you?" Mac asked.

Justin rolled his eyes. "As if." He threw the ball at the fence again and it went low into the bush. Instead of going to get it he turned to walk away.

"Hitting girls in the head with balls isn't how you get their attention," Mac called to his back.

Justin kept walking.

"Want to know how you get their attention?" Mac asked.

Justin stopped, but didn't turn around. Mac smiled to herself. So, he did like Maisy Walker.

"Buy her a chocolate to apologise at lunch."

"That's it?" Justin asked.

"No, that's not it," Mac said. "That's just the start."

Justin turned around but kept his eyes on the ground. "Then what?"

"Then ask her about her day. Find out what she's interested in and talk about that. Girls love being asked about themselves."

"What if she doesn't want to talk about her day?"

"Then at least you tried."

"Well that's stupid," Justin said. "Your advice sucks." He turned and leapt up the steps and disappeared into his house.

Mac walked back to the deck and climbed back into the hammock. At least she'd get an afternoon nap now.

Chapter 14

At work on Saturday morning, Stanley commented on how upbeat Mac seemed at work after her stint in hospital.

"It wasn't a heart attack, Stanley," Mac said.

"These doctors, they don't know anything nowadays," Stanley replied. "I'd get a second opinion."

"I'm dating a nurse, remember?" Mac replied. She folded down an apple box and tossed it into the recycling bin. "Actually, I haven't told you yet."

"Told me what?"

"Callie and I are engaged," Mac said. She was totally unprepared for Stanley's reaction. He lifted her off the ground in a bear hug and laughed.

"Mac! Congratulations. Hey, Maria," he called. "Maria!"

Maria poked her head out of the office. "What's the matter?"

"Mac's getting married!" he said.

Maria strode across the floor, her arms wide and wrapped Mac in a hug. "Oh, Mac. That's wonderful. When?" She pulled away and held Mac at arm's length. "When did she ask you?"

"I asked her, actually," Mac replied.

Stanley and Maria looked at each other and then back at Mac. Was it that hard to believe she'd popped the question?

"What?" Mac asked.

"Nothing, nothing. Congratulations," Stanley said. He headed over to the office.

"Where are you going?" Maria asked.

"To tell everyone," Stanley replied.

"No, Stanley, there's no need—" but Mac's pleas fell on deaf ears. Stanley told the whole shop the good news over the loudspeaker, and Mac's work mates and the shoppers in the store burst out into spontaneous applause. As embarrassed as Mac was right then, she actually felt pretty good. Getting engaged wasn't so bad after all.

She was still on cloud nine when she walked out of work that afternoon. As she got to her car, her phone rang. "Hey, Kate," she said. "I've been meaning to—"

"You need to get to the jeweller's right now," Kate said, without even saying hello first.

Mac stopped dead, her hand on the car door handle. "Why?"

"Callie's just walked in."

"How do you —?

"Doesn't matter. Just get there, Mac."

"On my way," Mac said, and hung up. Panic slowly rose in her chest and she fought the urge to speed. Why on earth would Callie be going to the jeweller?

❧

Mac swallowed hard as she pulled open the jewellery store door. Three heads turned to greet her as she entered and one of them wasn't happy. Callie's face was a mixture of confusion and sadness. The jeweller looked pleased to see Mac, as did the man standing beside Callie.

"Hey," Mac said, as she approached the counter. She leaned in to kiss Callie, but Callie turned her head so Mac got her on the cheek. "What are you doing here?" she whispered.

"I called to see how the ring was getting on," Callie replied, dead pan. "Gino asked if I wouldn't mind coming to the store so that *Mr* Mackenzie could thank us himself for returning it." There was an edge to her voice, and it didn't take an idiot to realise that Callie was containing her anger because they were in public.

"Oh," Mac said.

Mr Mackenzie grinned broadly and stuck out his hand. Mac shook it, but her arm felt like lead. "I'm so grateful," Mr Mackenzie said as he pumped Mac's hand. "I thought for sure it was gone but when Gino called me to say it had been returned, well, I was so happy."

"Good," Mac said.

"We're so sorry for the mix-up," Gino the jeweller said. "Two Mackenzies buying things at the same time. Who would've thought?" He shook his head and laughed.

"Huh," Mac said, apparently unable to utter anything more than single syllables.

"Well, we should get going," Callie said abruptly. "So glad it all worked out for you," she said to Mr Mackenzie, glaring at Mac.

"And you," Mr Mackenzie said.

Callie grabbed Mac by the arm and pulled her out of the store. When they got outside, Mac tried to calm Callie down.

"Callie, I'm—"

Callie put her hand up to stop Mac from talking. "We'll talk about it when we get home." She turned on her heels and walked away. Mac trudged back to her car and got in. She took a deep breath, started the car, and headed home.

Chapter 15

"It was an honest mistake," Mac said, following Callie up the hallway to the bedroom.

"An honest mistake is getting the wrong colour. An honest mistake is forgetting to take the pickles off the burger before you give it to someone."

"Come on, Cal, that was one time."

"Twice!" Callie replied, holding up two fingers just to make sure Mac got the point. "And don't you 'Come on Cal' me. There was nothing honest about any of what you did," Callie said as she tossed her shoes into her bag and turned and stomped out of the room. Mac followed her to the bathroom.

"I tried to tell you," Mac said. "It was just never the right time."

"The right time would have been as soon as I opened the present," Callie said. She flung open the cabinet and dumped toiletries into her bag.

"You're taking your toothbrush?"

Callie glared at Mac as she pushed past her to the lounge room. She dropped her bag on the floor next to a suitcase she'd already packed.

"You would've been upset if I'd told you it wasn't your present in front of my family," Mac said, trailing behind her.

"Like I'm upset now?"

"Exactly," Mac replied. Well that was the wrong answer.

Callie rounded on Mac. "I would've understood if you'd told me straight away but you had to string it out. String me out. And it wasn't just me. It was my family." Callie stabbed a finger at Mac. "And yours."

"But everything's changed," Mac pleaded. "I changed my mind. I do want to marry you."

"Oh, you changed your mind? Well that makes me feel so much better."

"Oh, good," Mac said. But the look on Callie's face said that was anything but good.

Callie sighed. "You didn't want to marry me in the first place, and that's what matters, Mac."

She wasn't yelling anymore. At least that was something. And Mac couldn't dispute the fact that she'd had no intention of marrying Callie before. But that was before everything had gotten crazy and Mac had had time to think on it. Mac wanted to marry Callie, she was sure of it, but now, Callie apparently didn't want to marry her back.

"How do I make you believe I'm serious?" Mac asked. She was hoping for a simple solution.

Callie let out a breath and looked at Mac with sad eyes. "I don't know, Mac," she said.

"Please," Mac pleaded. "Tell me what you need and I'll do it."

"I need time," Callie said. She picked up her bag and suitcase and walked to the door.

"Where are you going?" Mac asked in a last-ditch effort to hold off the inevitable.

Callie's hand hesitated on the doorknob and Mac thought for a moment that she might turn around and change her mind. "Home," she replied. Mac stood rooted to the spot as Callie walked through the door, and as she closed it behind her, shattered Mac's heart.

❧❧

Later that afternoon, Mac found herself sitting on her deck, holding a beer that she'd barely touched. After Callie had left, she called Kate, but had gotten her voice mail. She'd briefly considered calling her mother but decided against it. She wasn't ready to explain what had happened to her parents just yet and cop another round of 'What did you do to let this one go?' Instead, she wallowed in her self-made misery outside in the heat of the afternoon.

Mac didn't move when Justin started hitting a ball against the garage. What was the point? She didn't have the energy to take him on today. Then a ball came sailing over the fence and Mac watched it drop onto the grass. Soon after, Justin's head appeared over the top, and Mac watched, vaguely interested as he searched for the ball. She was pretty sure he couldn't see her, since she was tucked up near the back door behind the lattice screen.

Justin pulled himself over the fence and dropped onto the grass. He raced across the yard, retrieved his ball and then turned to leave. When Mac said, "Take the bucket" Justin froze like a hare caught in a spotlight, slowly turned to face Mac, his face changing from surprise to defiance. It almost made Mac want to laugh. Almost.

He stood, not moving, in the middle of the yard. Mac stood up, grabbed the bucket of balls she'd collected over the past year from under the BBQ bench and put it on the top step of the deck. "Take'em," she said.

Justin walked toward the deck, keeping his eyes on Mac. He picked up the bucket and turned to walk away. For whatever reason, he turned back and dropped the bucket. "What's wrong?" he asked.

"None of your business," Mac replied. She took a swig of her beer and grimaced. It had gotten warm. She hated warm beer.

Justin nodded. "Girl trouble, right?"

Mac looked at him. She had an overwhelming sense of deja vu. She nodded.

Justin tossed the tennis ball he had in his hand up into the air and caught it again. He did it twice more and then walked up onto the deck and sat on a chair at the other end of the table. "Girls," he said. "Enigmas."

Mac looked up, surprised. "Enigmas?"

"Yeah, like difficult to understand," Justin said. "Like Maxwell's batting."

"I know what an enigma is," Mac said. She was just surprised to discover that Justin knew what it was. Maybe he was smarter than he looked.

"What happened?" Justin asked.

"Callie and I are... taking a break," Mac explained.

"Too bad," Justin said. "I liked her."

"Me too," Mac replied.

"Why don't you go and get her back?" Justin asked.

Kids, Mac thought. Everything was so easy for them. "She doesn't want me to," Mac replied.

"She said that?"

"No, but I know that," Mac said.

Justin shrugged. "If she didn't say it, she didn't mean it."

Mac looked over at Justin. So naive. She didn't want to talk about Callie with Justin anymore. "How's your love life?" she asked.

Justin looked up grinned. "I did just what you said."

"You gave Maisy a chocolate?"

Justin nodded. "Bought her a Kit Kat."

"How'd that go?"

"She told me to rack off."

Mac snorted. "Sounds like you bombed."

"Yeah," Justin said. "But then Brook told me Kit Kats were her favourite, so it's all good."

Mac raised her eyebrows. "You're dating Brook now?"

Justin shrugged. "Don't know. I'm keeping my options open."

Mac shook her head. "That's not how it works."

"How does it work?" Justin asked.

"You spend some time together and see if you like each other. That's how it works at your age."

"What about your age?" Justin asked.

Mac narrowed her eyes. "Same thing, except it gets more expensive."

Justin grinned and Mac couldn't help but smile back. She wished it were that simple with Callie.

Mac watched as Justin flicked the ball around in his hands again. "You want someone to bowl at?" she asked.

Justin nodded. "Really?"

"Really," Mac replied. "Go set up some stumps down the side. I'll go inside and grab my bat and be out in a minute."

Justin leapt down the steps and disappeared around the side of the house. Mac headed inside to find her old Slazenger bat. On her way back outside, she checked her phone. Three missed calls from Kate, one from Sophie and none from Callie. She dropped the phone back onto the kitchen bench and pushed through the back door. Cracking some cricket balls with Justin might take her mind off things for a bit.

Chapter 16

Two days before Mac was due to fly out to Melbourne with Callie, she found herself sitting with Kate in a cafe, summoned for a pep talk of sorts. At least that's what it seemed like to Mac. She prodded at a limp piece of lettuce on her plate.

"I don't know why you don't just ask for no salad," Kate said.

"Because they pile it up with too many chips. I always feel bad sending uneaten chips back," Mac replied. What she didn't add was that Callie would normally pick at the extra chips off her plate when she ordered no salad, and she didn't want that thought to cross her mind right now. She didn't want to think about Callie at all, but it seemed the more she fought against it, the more Callie popped into her head.

"Maria said you're going back to work," Kate said, changing the subject. "You're not flying out to Melbourne?"

"What's the point?" Mac replied. "Callie obviously doesn't want me there."

"Did she say that?"

"She hasn't said anything."

"So, you're assuming," Kate said. She bit into her wrap and eyed Mac.

Mac sighed. "What else am I supposed to think, Kate? I've left messages for her and she hasn't gotten back to me. I'm just going to leave her alone. If she wants me back, she knows where I am."

Kate placed her wrap down onto her plate and wiped her hands on a napkin. "So that's it, is it? You're just going to let her walk away?"

"You sound like my mother," Mac replied.

"So I bloody should," Kate said.

Mac looked up. It was rare for Kate to lose her cool about anything. "What do you expect me to do? Chase her to Melbourne?"

"Yes," Kate said. "That's exactly what I think you should do."

"It'll just be a total waste of time. She won't even answer my phone calls."

Kate huffed out a breath. "You'd think you'd know more about girls, since you're actually one yourself. Though sometimes I do wonder."

Mac dropped her fork onto her plate. "What's that supposed to mean?"

"We want you to make an effort, Mac."

"I have."

Kate scoffed. "You have not. This is the first time you've left the house since Callie left and you couldn't have made less of an effort." She waved a hand in Mac's general direction.

Mac looked down at her t-shirt. "What's wrong with what I'm wearing?"

"Nothing," Kate said. "Except you look like you haven't slept or showered in a week. You could've at least done your hair."

"I need a haircut," Mac retorted, which was the truth. She didn't tell Kate she was right about the not sleeping bit though. She'd gotten so used to Callie being in the bed beside her, it had been hard for her to get any sleep at all. The first night after Callie had left, Mac woke thinking Callie was in bed beside her, only to discover it was a pillow wedged up against her back.

"Sort yourself out, Mac," Kate said. "And go and talk to Callie."

"What if she doesn't want to?"

"Then at least you tried."

And there it was. Mac's own words to Justin just a few days before being thrown back at her. She'd told Justin how easy it would be. Why on earth couldn't she believe it about talking to Callie? "I'll think about it," Mac said, picking a chip off her plate and shoving it into her mouth.

Chapter 17

The day Mac and Callie were due to fly out to Melbourne came and although Mac told herself she should go to the airport anyway, because Callie hadn't specifically told Mac she didn't want her to go, Mac went to work instead.

Mac had taken Kate's advice and gone to Callie's apartment, but she wasn't there and when she got home and found Callie's plane ticket gone, it was obvious she'd run away to Melbourne. Mac had really stuffed up if Callie couldn't even stand to be in the same city as her.

If Callie wanted space, then that was what Mac was going to give her. How much space, Mac had no idea. What Mac did know, a week out from Christmas, was that with Sophie away and Kate enamoured with Andy, her Christmas was going to suck big time. And as if things couldn't get worse, her grandmother's ring had been delivered that morning. Mac had stashed it in her bedside table, the packaging unopened.

Mac spent the morning at work out the back of the shop so she didn't have to talk to customers. Stanley had insisted she take the holidays she'd arranged anyway, but Mac knew moping around home would do nothing for her mood. She'd much rather be busy at work than be alone at home. She was ticking off deliveries out the back of the shop when Andy appeared at the loading dock. He wasn't in his uniform, so Mac figured it wasn't a work visit. He ambled over and picked up an orange from a box beside Mac and held it to his nose. He went to put it back into the box, but Mac said, "You may as well have that."

Andy smiled and pocketed the orange. "Thanks."

"What do you want?" Mac asked, turning and walking over to a pallet of watermelons.

Andy followed her. "To apologise."

"What for?"

"I feel a bit responsible for you and Callie," Andy said. "It was sort of my stuff up. I'm a courier guy. I should be delivering the right packages."

Mac shrugged. It was far too late for apologies and as much as she really wanted to blame Andy, or anyone else for that matter, this was all on her. "Forget it," Mac said.

"No, really. It's a huge stuff-up. Getting things right is something my company prides itself on."

"Your company?" Mac asked.

"Yeah. I own Rapid Couriers," he said with a smile. When Mac didn't answer, he said, "Anyway, Kate told me about your talk."

Great, Mac thought. Now they're telling each other everything. She moved over to a pallet of mangoes.

"You were supposed to fly out today," Andy tried again. "Is that still happening?"

"Even if I wanted to, I missed my flight."

"You could get another one," Andy suggested.

Mac shrugged as she moved to another pallet of fruit.

"Look, I really am sorry, and I do want to make it up to you. Here," he dug into his pocket and pulled out a card. "Anything you need, give me a call."

Mac took the card. "Thanks."

"I better get going," Andy said. "Last minute Christmas shopping with Kate."

Mac nodded. Andy waved awkwardly and then turned and walked away. Mac looked at the business card. 'Rapid Couriers. Anything, anywhere, anytime, on time.' She shoved it into her back pocket and got back to work.

❧

Later that night, Mac sat on the lounge flicking through channels on the TV. Every one of them had something about Christmas on it. She sighed and turned it off. She looked down at the Christmas tree, where one lonely present sat. The key rings. How had everything gone so wrong? All Mac wanted was for Callie to move in with her and be a part of her life full time. Now that might never happen.

She slumped back in the chair and looked at the ceiling. She thought about what Kate had said. Would Callie really want Mac to chase after her? Mac didn't know anymore. She'd grown so used to having Callie around, the thought of not being with her had never crossed her mind. Now she faced that very real prospect if she didn't do something about it.

Mac let out a long breath. Then she stood up and walked over to the fridge to get another beer. As she opened the door, she knocked a magnet off along with some paperwork. She picked it up and as she went to put it back, she realised what it was. She turned it over in her hand. It was the cricket ticket Callie's parents had sent, but instead of two, there was just one. Mac knelt down on the floor and looked under the fridge. The other one wasn't under there, and it hadn't dropped anywhere on the floor that she could see. That could mean only one thing.

Callie had deliberately left it behind. Maybe Kate was right. Justin too. Maybe Callie did want Mac to chase after her. If she didn't want her to, she wouldn't have let her keep the cricket ticket. She snatched her plane ticket off the bench and called the booking line. After talking the woman in the call centre into letting her have credit for her missed flight, less some fees, Mac requested a new flight.

"As soon as possible," she said.

Mac heard typing on the other end of the phone and then the woman came back and said, "Your new ticket will cost $2,500."

"Two thou—." Mac couldn't believe it. Even with the credit from her original ticket it was going to cost her over $2,000 just to get to Melbourne. "Why so much?"

"We only have business class available on the next available flights," the operator explained. "And it's Christmas. You shouldn't have missed your first flight."

Mac sighed. What was two grand when you were trying to win the love of your life back? "Just give me a minute. I'll get my credit card."

Mac walked over to the side table and picked up her wallet. When she pulled her credit card out, a business card came out with it. *'Anything, anywhere, anytime, on time'* it said. Mac turned her attention back to her phone. "On second thoughts, I'll just take the credit."

She hung up and dialled the number on the card. "Andy? It's Mac. That slogan on your business card, is it just a slogan? Or do you deliver anything, anytime, anywhere?"

Chapter 18

At 5.30am the next morning, Mac climbed out of a taxi in front of the Rapid Couriers depot. It was a massive warehouse building just off the motorway and it buzzed with activity. Andy told her to come straight through to the back office when she arrived, since the front office wouldn't be open until nine. Mac asked a man in hi-vis for directions and was pointed through to the back left of the warehouse and was told to follow the yellow safety line.

Mac looked around the cavernous interior as she made her way to the back. She couldn't think of the last time she felt so small. Massive shelves full of boxes took up most of the space, and she walked alongside two rows of wooden pallets stacked with more boxes wrapped in clear plastic wrap. The courier company was much bigger than Mac imagined.

When she reached the back office, she knocked on the door. Andy looked up from his desk, smiled and beckoned her in.

"Mac," he said standing up walking around the desk. "Coffee?" he offered, walking to a small cabinet set against the wall.

"Thanks," Mac replied. "Love one."

"Help yourself," he said. "Though you might want to grab one of our refillable cups so you can take it with you. You'll need a bit of caffeine with the trip you're taking today." He looked at his watch. "Barry should be almost finished loading, so he'll want to get going soon."

Mac poured herself a coffee into a Rapid Couriers branded refillable cup, stirred in some milk and sugar and capped it with a lid. Andy made one of his own and lead Mac back outside into the depot, and then out the back into the early morning sunshine.

"Kate never mentioned your company was so big," Mac said, sipping on her coffee.

"It's not that big, really," Andy replied. "We're mostly local but we use other small local couriers to get stuff around in other states."

Mac followed Andy around to a yard at the back where a line of trucks sat parked. One of them was sitting out, a shortish round man standing beside it, looking at a clipboard.

"Hey, Barry," Andy said as they approached.

Barry looked up and smiled. "Hey, boss. This my last package?"

Andy laughed. "This is she." He introduced them and said, "Barry'll be your tour guide to Tamworth this morning."

Mac shook Barry's hand. "Thanks for taking me."

"No dramas," Barry replied. "Be good to have some company for the trip."

"You're ready to go?" Andy asked Barry.

Barry nodded.

Andy looked to Mac. "I'll leave you in Barry's capable hands. He'll pass you on at Tamworth. Give me a call if you need anything."

"Thanks," Mac replied.

Andy walked back to the warehouse and Mac turned her attention back to Barry.

"Right," Barry said. "Hop in."

He opened the passenger door for Mac, who tossed her bag inside and climbed up. Once she was in with her seatbelt on, Barry climbed up into the driver's seat. "Hope you don't mind a bit of Acca Dacca," he said as he turned the truck on and drove out of the depot.

"Acca Dacca is fine," Mac replied as she settled into her seat, the opening riffs of *Highway to Hell* seeing them on her first leg of her trip to Melbourne.

Barry turned out to be a bit of an Aussie music fan. Even at his age, which he said was north of fifty but didn't say how far, he still listened to Triple J. Had done for years. He could talk himself out of a wet paper bag too, which was fine by Mac, because Barry didn't ask too many questions about her. She was totally fine with that. She didn't want to go into the reasons behind her trip to Melbourne, and Barry, thankfully, didn't ask. She was grateful for the time to be able to come up with a plan to get Callie back. So far, she had nothing.

They arrived in Tamworth just after 1pm. Barry told Mac she wasn't due to leave until 2pm and gave her directions for the shopping centre nearby. "Be back by ten to two," Barry said. "Dave doesn't like to wait around."

Mac nodded and went off in search of lunch.

The second leg of Mac's trip took her past Christmas decorations, drooping in the heat, and bales of hay made to look like Santa and his reindeer. If she thought Barry was a talker, he was nothing on Dave. He droned on and on about the football, which took Mac almost an hour to realise he meant Aussie Rules and not Rugby League. The conversation was interrupted occasionally by Dave jumping in on random conversations on the two-way radio and those were the times she lay her head against the window and pretended to sleep. She didn't realise how exhausting being a passenger in a truck could be. Although she did think Dave's monotone drone could put anyone to sleep.

By the time they arrived in Dubbo, Mac's head was throbbing from a headache, and she didn't even get the chance to grab a bite to eat before she was in the cab of the next truck. They stopped at a truck stop in Parkes for tea and after almost five hours of country music,

Mac was deposited at 10.30pm at a small depot just outside of Wagga Wagga.

Her final driver, Trevor, apologised as soon as he introduced himself. "We're a bit late loading," he said. "Won't get away for another hour or so yet."

Mac sighed.

"Important trip?" Trevor asked.

"Yeah," Mac said. "But I guess we get there when we get there."

"True enough," Trevor replied. "Sometimes you just can't help being late." He beckoned her into the office and offered her a seat. Then he busied himself preparing coffees. "Want one?"

Mac nodded. "Thanks. White and one." She'd had a few hours sleep on the last leg but truck cabs weren't the comfiest places in the world, so she'd discovered. She could do with a sleep now, but she'd have to wait until the next leg was underway and hope that Trevor's truck was more comfortable.

"Had dinner?" Trevor asked, handing Mac a mug. "The missus made me a big roast meal. I've still got some left in my hot box if you want some."

"Thanks, but I'm good. We stopped back in Parkes," Mac replied.

Trevor smiled. "Bruce and his meat pies from the BP." He shook his head and sat in the chair across from her. "He's supposed to be on a diet, you know. Did he tell you that?"

Mac nodded. "While he was drinking his second Red Bull."

Trevor chuckled into his coffee. "So, what's taking you to Melbourne?"

Mac sipped her coffee and thought about why she was doing something as crazy as getting into trucks with strangers. She opted for the short version. "I did something stupid and I'm hoping I can make up for it."

Trevor nodded knowingly. "Relationship trouble, hey?"

"You could say that," Mac replied.

"How big was the stupid?" Trevor asked.

"Pretty big," Mac replied.

"No wonder you didn't just send flowers."

Mac shook her head and smiled in spite of herself. "No amount of flowers will make up for what I did."

"Hence the big road trip," Trevor said.

"Exactly," Mac replied.

"So what's your plan once you get there?"

Mac shrugged. "No idea. I'm just hoping she's still talking to me."

"Well, once she finds out you've spent over a full day in trucks just to get to her, she might be happier to talk to you."

"I hope so," Mac replied.

Trevor drained his coffee and stood up. "I better go check on my load. Feel free to hang out here. Have more coffee, a snooze on the couch. I'll come grab you when we're ready to go."

"Thanks," Mac replied.

Trevor tapped a finger on the desk. "We'll get your girl back, don't you worry."

Chapter 19

About two hours into the trip, Trevor turned down the radio and said, "Is this your first trip to Melbourne?"

Mac nodded.

"It's where your girl lives?" Trevor asked.

"Her family," Mac replied. "We were supposed to visit them for Christmas, but we had a huge fight and she came down here without me."

"Must've been a hell of a fight," Trevor said.

He didn't take his eyes off the road, but Mac could see his face had softened and his tone wasn't judgmental at all. She got the feeling he'd had a couple of fights like hers and Callie's himself.

"You know," Trevor said, scratching his chin. "I had a blue with Evie– that's my wife –

like that once."

"Oh?"

"Yep. Massive one. She wanted to settle down and buy a house and get married and all that malarky, but me?" Trevor huffed. "I was young and thought I knew everything. But what did I know, hey?"

"But you married her though?" Mac said.

Trevor snorted. "Not until thirty years later."

Mac whistled. "Thirty years. That's a long time to make her wait." Even Mac knew that was stupid.

"Ha! She didn't wait for me!" Trevor said.

"She didn't?"

Trevor shook his head. "Went and married some other fella, had a couple of kids."

"What did you do?" Mac asked.

"Well," Trevor said. "I went off and worked on oil rigs for a bit, and then I went overseas, bumming around. Almost got married twice." He glanced at Mac. "Glad I didn't because hoo boy would they have been mistakes."

Mac couldn't help but laugh at Trevor's simple self-reflection. He was so matter-of-fact, it made Mac think about her and Callie and how uncomplicated life was between them. About how complicated the last two weeks had been while Mac had been twisting herself in knots trying to keep herself from making the one commitment that would either make or break their relationship, before she finally broke it anyway.

"So what happened?" Mac asked.

Trevor's face broke out in one of those wistful smiles Mac had seen on her mum whenever her and her dad talked about the past. "I'd just started working for this mob, eleven years ago tomorrow. Just south of Albury-Wodonga on my way up to Wagga Wagga when a tire blew on the car in front. I pulled over to give them a hand and when I saw who got out of the car, well, you could've knocked me down with a feather."

"It was Evie?"

Trevor nodded. "She hadn't changed a bit." He sighed. "Me, though." He laughed and patted his belly. "Few too many beers and pies, but she still recognised me. I drove her into town, and we chatted like no time had gone at all."

"Wow," Mac said. "So, you got back together after all that time?"

"Not right away," Trevor said. "She made me work for it, did Evie." He chuckled and let out a breath. "An independent woman doesn't care whether you stay or go, but if you stay, you have to be there a hundred percent."

"So what made you stay?"

"She let me," Trevor said. "See, the key is, she didn't need me. She still loved me, after all those years, but she didn't need me anymore. And I realised, after all that time away from her, that she was the one person I'd ever missed in my whole life."

Mac smiled and Trevor smiled back. "I don't ever want to miss another day with her again. And that's why—" He patted an envelope on the dashboard. "—she's getting this for Christmas."

"What is it?" Mac asked.

"My severance pay," Trevor replied.

"You lost your job?" Mac asked.

"Took a redundancy," Trevor said. "The company's restructuring and they offered voluntary redundancies, and Evie and me have been talking about taking that long, slow trip around the country, so..." He shrugged and then winked. "She doesn't know about it yet. I wanted to surprise her."

"She won't be mad?" Mac asked. She was sure Callie would be furious with her if Mac made a decision like that without her.

Trevor chuckled. "She's been at me to retire early for years. And just between you and me, I've already missed so much time with her, I don't want to miss any more."

Mac smiled and nodded. Even though it had only been a bit over a week, she'd missed having Callie around the house. She'd missed waking up to notes in the morning when Callie had started an early shift and left before Mac had gotten out of bed. She missed Callie snuggling into her back at night when she got home late. The house had been empty and lifeless without her in it and Mac realised that for all her doubts about committing to Callie, she didn't want to be like Trevor and miss out on some of the best years of her life with the person she loved most in the world.

"Thanks," Mac said. "For everything."

"You're welcome," Trevor said. "You're my last ever delivery." He glanced at Mac and grinned. "What a way to finish up. Evie's gonna love this story."

Chapter 20

Twenty-two hours, ten cups of coffee, a meat pie, packet of Skittles and four hours of broken sleep after she started, Mac finally arrived in Melbourne. She'd barely been able to sleep during the last leg, probably due to the caffeine and sugar overload, and she'd been grateful for Trevor's intermittent chatter on everything from politics to the cricket, and his pretty frank assessment of marriage.

Mac had scrolled through Sophie's photos on Facebook, finding herself missing her friends and wishing this Christmas was just like any other, with the three of them, plus Callie, having a big Christmas lunch together. She wondered if she'd have a chance to see Sophie before she flew out, since they were all in Melbourne at the same time, and since she'd probably need a shoulder to cry on if Callie didn't take her back.

Mac considered going to the airport to see Sophie before she flew out, since they were now in the same city again, but decided against it. Sophie didn't need to be hearing about Mac's problems before she was about to jet off on the trip of a lifetime. She sent Sophie an early Christmas message on Facebook instead, hoping she'd get it before she flew out that afternoon. She sent a quick message to Kate to let her know she'd arrived safely and got a thumbs up and 'good luck with Callie' back.

The truck rolled into the depot in Dandenong just after 4am, and it took Mac a few minutes of stretching and walking around to work out the stiffness in her body.

"We just have to unload and then I'll be heading home. If you want to wait another hour or so, I can drop you somewhere," Trevor said.

"I think I'll be fine. I just need to know how to get to Callie's."

"Where are you heading?" Trevor asked as he pulled on a high-vis vest and gloves.

Mac pulled her phone from her pocket. Still nothing from Callie. She dug into her bag and pulled out the envelope that had her cricket ticket in. She flipped it over to look at the return address on the back. "Toorak," she said.

Trevor whistled. "Your girl's got money."

"Why do you say that?" Mac asked.

"Multi-million-dollar places over there," Trevor said. He wrote something on his clipboard. "You haven't been there before?"

"I haven't met her family yet."

"Gees, what a way to meet them, hey?"

"I know," Mac said. "How do I get there from here?"

"You'll need to take the train into South Yarra, then either the train or taxi from there, depending on where you're going," Trevor said. "Are you sure I can't drop you off? It's only a bit out of my way."

Mac smiled. "Thanks, but you should get home to Evie. I'll be fine."

She left with instructions on how to get to the train station, and once she had her ticket and was sitting waiting for the train, she sent Kate a text to let her know she'd arrived safely. She thought about texting Andy, but figured Kate would let him know, if Trevor hadn't already.

◦◦◦

Mac hadn't realised how hungry she was until she could smell the brewing coffee as she walked out into the early morning sunshine at the South Yarra Station.

She knew it was probably a bad idea to have more coffee, but she bought one anyway, along with a toasted ham and cheese sandwich, and ate it as she walked the rest of the way to Callie's parent's house. Google maps told her it would take a little over half an hour to get to her destination and although it was still early morning, she could feel the heat starting to creep in as the sun began to rise.

She made her way down the main street, past more cafes and closed shops that reminded her of some of the more affluent suburbs at home. It was a lot quieter than she guessed it would be once they all started opening for the day.

By the time she'd turned down Callie's parents' street, Mac's heart was beating overtime. Sweat trickled down her back as she wandered down the tree-lined street, gaping in awe at the size of the houses. Trevor was right. They practically screamed money.

She walked past perfectly trimmed hedges, impossibly green lawns and stark white facades. She'd never felt under-dressed walking down a street before.

Finally, she reached the front of Callie's house and stood staring up at a bright white three-story mansion, the white so bright she had to shield her eyes. A wrought iron gate stood between Mac and the front door. She stepped up and peered inside. The gardens were immaculate, with green balled shrubs bordering a bright green lawn. They all looked so perfect; Mac wondered if they weren't fake. Callie had never mentioned that her parents were loaded.

Mac tried the gate, but it was locked and she spied a security panel on the wall to the side. She thought about pressing the buzzer but decided it was probably best to wait until a more respectable time. It wouldn't be a great first introduction to Callie's family if she woke them up so early.

She considered calling Callie, that would only give her a chance to refuse to see her. She glanced around the empty street and, without anything better to do, or anywhere else to go, she sat down on the step under the entrance, and leaned her back onto the wall to wait.

Mac hadn't realised how tired she was until she sat down. It was hard to imagine a concrete step would be more comfortable than a truck seat, but once Mac was sitting down again, her whole body relaxed. She decided to close her eyes, for just a minute, her last thoughts about how lucrative the party planning business must be.

❧

Mac was woken by the earth shaking around her. She groggily opened her eyes, trying to get her bearings. How long had she been asleep? And more importantly, where was she? She squinted against the sunlight at two shadows standing above her.

"Up," a voice ordered.

"What?" Mac asked, still trying to get her bearings. She was finding it hard to focus.

"Come on," the voice said. "You can't stay here."

Mac looked around and remembered where she was. She squinted up at the people in front of her and realised they were police officers.

"What's going on?" she asked.

"You're trespassing," one of the officers replied. "You need to move on."

"My girlfriend lives here," Mac said, struggling to clear the cotton wool that had apparently lodged itself in her head.

"Yeah right," said the other officer. "What have you taken?"

"Taken?" Mac asked, confused.

"Drugs," the taller officer said. He knelt down and looked into her face. "She's high, I reckon. See how red her eyes are?"

"What? No," Mac replied.

The officers ignored her and lifted her to her feet. "Come on. We'll get you sobered up."

"I'm not high," Mac replied, trying to struggle out of their grip, but they held tight.

"Don't struggle or we'll charge you with resisting arrest," one of the officers said.

That was the last thing she needed so she let them lead her to their car. "Where are you taking me?" she asked as they helped her into the back seat.

"Normally we'd drop you at a shelter," the taller officer said. "But they're full, being Christmas. So we'll let you sleep it off in one of the cells."

"You're taking me to jail?" Mac asked.

The officer laughed and shook his head. "Just to the station."

As they drove away, the officer sitting in front of her in the passenger seat asked, "Is there anyone we can call for you?"

"No," Mac replied. She leaned back into the seat and closed her eyes. At least a police cell might have a bed she could finally get some sleep on.

Chapter 21

After sleeping most of the day away in a police cell, Mac was let go with a warning. She collected her bag and as she headed out the door of the station into the late afternoon sunshine, a familiar voice stopped her cold.

"The things you do for attention, Mac."

Mac turned to see Callie, standing with her arms crossed over her chest, one of her disappointed looks on her face.

"What are you doing here?" Mac asked.

"What do you think?"

"I didn't ask them to call you," Mac said.

"Your mother did," Callie replied.

"My mother? But—"

"She got a phone call from the police to say they'd picked you up in Melbourne."

"I asked them not to call anyone," Mac said.

"What did you think they'd do?" Callie asked. "Let you stay in jail?"

"No," Mac replied, sullen.

"They called your mother to make sure you weren't homeless."

"And then she called you?"

Callie nodded. "Only after she panicked and called you back a few times and couldn't understand why a police officer kept answering your phone."

Mac shook her head. That sounded exactly like something her mother would do.

"The question is," Callie said, walking to the door and pushing it open. "What are you doing here?"

Mac followed Callie outside and squinted at the brightness. "I came to see you."

"That doesn't explain what you're doing getting yourself arrested." Callie strode through the car park and Mac had to jog just to keep up.

"I didn't get arrested," Mac replied.

"Well, would you care to tell me why the hell I needed to come all the way down here this morning just to get you out of jail?"

"I wasn't in jail," Mac replied. Callie turned and narrowed her eyes. "They thought I was high or something and put me in a cell to sober up," Mac said.

"Jesus, Mac. Really?"

"I wasn't high, Callie," Mac said. "Maybe from caffeine and sugar. Can you get high on caffeine and sugar?"

Callie let out a breath and stopped and turned. "Stop lying to me, Mac. I'm over your lies."

"I'm not lying, Callie, I promise," Mac pleaded. "Just, listen. I talked Andy into letting me use his courier service to get down to Melbourne from Brissy."

"Wait a minute. Who's Andy?"

"Kate's boyfriend," Mac said. "Doesn't matter. Anyway, I hardly slept a wink the whole way here and by the time I got to your parents' house, it must've all caught up to me."

"My parents' house? You went to my parents' house?"

Mac nodded.

"Why on earth would you do that?"

"I told you. I wanted to see you."

Callie's face changed from confused to amused. Mac felt that might be at least a little bit of progress. At least Callie didn't seem angry anymore. Callie shook her head. "You're an idiot, Mac, you know that?" She turned and started walking again.

Mac followed behind. "Me? Why?"

"I wasn't even in Melbourne," Callie replied over her shoulder.

It was Mac's turn to be confused. "You weren't?"

Callie stopped behind a sleek black BMW. "No. What on earth made you think I was?"

"You said you were going home," Mac replied.

"When?"

"When we had that big argument last week."

Callie tilted her head and frowned. "I meant my apartment, Mac. Not Melbourne." She knocked on the boot of the car and it slowly popped open. "Put your bag in and get in the car."

Mac tossed her bag into the boot and closed it down. "Wait. Whose car is this?"

"Anthony's," Callie replied.

"Your brother knows?"

Callie didn't answer. She said, "He picked us up from the airport."

"Us? But—" Mac's head was spinning, although that could just be the caffeine withdrawal. "Wait, so you weren't in Melbourne?"

Callie tapped her foot impatiently. "I just told you that."

"And you flew in this morning?"

"Yes, Mac, I flew in this morning."

Mac let out a breath. She'd come to Melbourne for nothing. "Does your family know? About us?"

Callie turned and stabbed the air in front of Mac with her finger. "As far as my family knows, you and I flew in this morning and Anthony picked us up from the airport. Got it?"

"What about Anthony? Does he know?"

"That he didn't pick you up from the airport? I think you're smart enough to know the answer to that." Callie opened the car door.

"No, I mean about us," Mac said.

"Yes, he knows," Callie said, and she slid into the passenger's seat and closed the door.

Mac opened the back door and got in.

"Hey, Mac," Anthony said. "How's things?"

"Oh, you know," Mac replied. She saw him wink at her in the rear-view mirror and was pretty sure he did know.

On the upside, Callie was at least talking to her now, though Mac was curious as to why she'd lie to her family. Mac's phone buzzed in her pocket. She pulled it out and looked at the screen. It was her mother. Even though she wanted to ignore it, she figured she may as well get the phone call out of the way. "Hello, Mum," she answered. "No, I'm not in jail."

Callie turned in her seat to look at Mac, and the look on her face told Mac she'd get no sympathy for what she was about to cop from her mother.

Chapter 22

Mac was grateful for her phone running out of battery in the middle of her mother's lecture. She knew she was going to cop the rest of it as soon as she turned her phone back on, and probably a whole other phone call from her father too. There were missed calls and messages from Kate and Sophie that dinged through while she was talking to her mother, but since her phone was dead, she'd have to deal with them later. For now, she just had to worry about what she'd say to Callie to get her back.

Anthony turned the car into the side street beside Callie's parent's house. They waited as the garage door slid up and then he drove in and closed the door behind them.

"Get your stuff," Callie ordered, and Mac did as she was told.

"I'll tell Mum and Dad you wanted to freshen up," Anthony said.

"Thanks," Callie replied. "We'll be down soon."

Mac followed Callie through a side door to a path outside. They walked down the side of the house, turned a corner and along a breezeway that connected the house to another building with a wall full of windows. The entry opened into a combined kitchen, dining and lounge area and it all opened up onto a timber deck that overlooked the pool.

"Is this a granny flat?" Mac asked, dropping her bag on the floor. She followed Callie over to the kitchen.

"It's the guest house," Callie replied.

"What's the difference?" Mac asked.

Callie pulled two glasses down from a cupboard and filled them with water. "Guest houses are for short stays," Callie replied, pushing a glass of water across to Mac.

"I could really do with a beer if you have one."

"You don't get to have beer after you've been hopped up on caffeine and sugar," Callie replied. "Drink your water."

Mac did as she was told, figuring it was best not to pick this battle when there was a much bigger one to come. "Don't you have a room in the house?"

Callie shrugged. "Of course I do, but there's more privacy here."

Mac thought there was more to that story but decided not to push it. As she was finishing her glass of water, Callie's phone buzzed. She looked at it and Mac detected a hint of annoyance. "Go and have a shower," she said.

"Don't you want to talk?" Mac asked.

Callie's head snapped up. "Of course I want to talk."

Mac could sense the tension.

Callie took a breath. "Sorry. It'll have to wait until later."

"How much later," Mac asked. "Shouldn't we get it out of the way?"

Callie put down her phone. "Mac, can you just please go and have a shower?"

"Fine," Mac said. She walked over and picked up her bag from the entry. She hadn't seen Callie this tense before. Callie didn't even get this upset over work, even when she was tired from night shift.

"Do you have anything decent to wear?" Callie asked.

"Decent how?" Mac asked.

"Something that's not jersey or sport-oriented?" Callie replied. "Or shorts," she added.

"Like going out clothes?" Mac asked.

The corner of Callie's mouth twitched up. "Yes, like going out clothes."

"I brought my good jeans and a button up shirt," Mac replied.

Callie nodded. "That'll have to do for now, but we'll have to find you something better to wear before tonight."

"What's happening tonight?" Mac asked.

Callie let out a breath. "My parents are throwing us an engagement party."

Mac's jaw dropped open. "But—"

Callie rolled her eyes. "I know, but this is what they do, Mac. Can you just go and get cleaned up so we can get the first stage over with?"

"The first stage?" *There are stages to an engagement party?* Mac wondered.

"You have to meet my family before the party," Callie said. She dropped onto the lounge and started unlacing her shoes. "We won't have to stay for long and then you and I," she said, pausing to look at Mac for effect. "Can come back here and talk."

Mac let out a breath. She'd only done the 'meet the parent's' thing once before and that had ended in disaster. Of course, it was highly unlikely, given the sort of house Callie's parents lived in, that they were extremely competitive Uno players like her last girlfriend's family were. Mac couldn't imagine what sorts of things rich people were into, but she was fairly sure board games weren't top of the list. And the fact that Callie was so uptight about seeing them didn't give Mac a lot of confidence. It also didn't help that Callie hadn't actually been up front about her family's money.

Callie stood up and directed Mac to the bathroom, full of white tiles and marble and gave her ten minutes to be ready. Mac caught a glimpse of herself in the massive mirror above the double sink. She looked like death warmed up. No wonder Callie snuck her in through the garage.

⁓

By the time Mac finished in the bathroom, Callie had changed into a white and yellow sun dress and styled her hair. Mac's heart leapt straight to her throat. After a week of not seeing Callie, or talking to her, she looked amazing. She was standing in front of the windows looking out, and she turned when she heard Mac enter the room. She looked Mac up and down and nodded approvingly.

"That's much better than before," Callie said.

"I feel under-dressed compared to you. I would've brought my good pants if I'd known your family was so fancy."

Callie's eyes darkened, just a touch, but enough for Mac to notice. She turned away and said, "We better get going, or we won't hear the end of it. Mum hates it when people are late."

They walked back down the same path but took a right turn before they got to the garage. Callie stopped at the bottom of the steps and looked at Mac.

"Remember," she said. "Everything's fine between us."

"I know," Mac replied, wishing it weren't a lie.

"And just—"

"Don't embarrass you?" Mac finished.

Callie gave Mac a smile that seemed tinged with, what? Sadness? Tiredness? Mac couldn't quite put her finger on it and without thinking, she grabbed Callie's hand and gave it a squeeze. Callie looked down at Mac's fingers entwined through hers and for a moment, Mac thought she'd pull away, but she didn't. She said, "Just be yourself."

After what Callie had said earlier, Mac wasn't sure being herself was the best advice. She nodded anyway and followed Callie across the terrace, where high tables with crisp white tablecloths had been set out. The bulbs from string lights in the tree and bushes glittered in the sunlight, and garden chairs had been placed just so around the manicured garden.

Mac leaned in close to Callie and whispered, "How many people are coming?"

"I have no idea," Callie replied. She paused in front of a set of bright white French doors and huffed out a breath. "Ready?"

Mac wasn't sure if Callie was talking to herself or not, but she answered, "Let's do it."

Callie turned and opened her mouth like she wanted to say something, but she bit her lip and simply nodded. Her grip on Mac's hand had tightened and her shoulders had stiffened.

Before she could stop herself, Mac blurted out, "I love you."

Callie's shoulders relaxed but she didn't reply. She opened the door and led Mac inside.

Chapter 23

As soon as they entered the room, Anthony presented Mac a choice between beer and champagne. Mac chose the beer. "You're going to need this," Anthony said quietly, clapping her on the shoulder.

"Welcome to the mad house," Callie's other brother, Mark, said, taking a swig of his own beer. Mac sipped on her beer and let Callie lead her across the room to where Callie's parents looked like they were having one of those arguments that weren't meant to look like arguments.

Callie's dad, in tan long pants and a light blue polo shirt, leaned on a black marble mantlepiece. His back was turned and he was talking to a woman in a white dress who looked just like Callie, only older. It had to be Callie's mum. Mac had only ever seen them in photos. They turned, and when they saw Mac and Callie, Callie's dad smiled and gave Callie a hug.

Callie's mum stood back, her face pinched like she'd just sucked on something sour.

"No ring," was the first thing Callie's mum said.

"Oh, it's—" Mac started.

"—getting resized," Callie finished and then introduced Mac.

Callie's dad shook Mac's hand and Callie's mum forced a smile but made no effort to show affection to Mac or Callie.

"It's nice to finally meet you, Mr and Mrs Preston," Mac said.

"Ryan, please," Callie's dad said. "You're practically family now."

Mac noticed Callie's mum didn't ask to be called by her first name. She switched her gaze from Mac to Callie. "I'm glad you decided to put family over work for once. It's preposterous that anyone should have to work over Christmas."

"I work at a hospital, mum. Holidays are our busiest times," Callie replied flatly.

"Yes. Well, it's not like you're a doctor. Anyway, I'm glad you managed to change your flights at the last minute. Lord knows why you didn't just say no to to taking on extra shifts when you were supposed to be on holidays." Before Callie had a chance to respond, her mother continued. "Although I wish you'd have given us more time to organise this engagement party. Half of our friends are away for Christmas."

Callie's shoulders stiffened. "It was your idea to have the party, Mum. I said we were happy to wait until the New Year so Mac's family could be here."

"Nonsense," Callie's mum said. "I'm sure Mackenzie's happy to not have to organise it, right, Mackenzie? This is, after all, what we do." She swept her hand across the room dramatically.

"Er, sure, Mrs Preston."

"After not being included in the proposal, it's the least we can do," Callie's mum went on.

"Mum—" Callie warned.

Mac pulled at her collar. It had gotten stuffy inside all of a sudden.

"I mean if we'd known you were going to propose, Mackenzie," Callie's mum said, apparently oblivious to Callie's glare. "We could have made it special."

"Not everything has to be planned," Callie said. "And it was special." She dropped Mac's hand. "I need a drink." To Mac, she leaned in and said quietly, "I'll be back in a minute."

Callie walked away leaving Mac stranded with Ryan and her mum. "So, er, thanks for the Christmas present. I'm really looking forward to watching the cricket."

Ryan grinned. "Callie said you're a mad cricket fan. We go to the MCG more for the football, but we always go on Boxing Day. It's great networking for the business."

Mark joined in the conversation. "Who do you barrack for?" he asked, sidling over and standing beside Mac.

"Barrack?"

"Football," Mark replied. "Please don't tell us you're a Collingwood supporter."

Mac racked her brain to try to work out who Mark was talking about and then she realised the football they were talking about was AFL and not rugby league. Mac didn't watch AFL. In fact, she knew as much about AFL as she did carpentry, which was exactly nothing.

"You're talking about AFL," Mac said.

"What other football is there?" Mark asked.

"Don't be an arse," Anthony said, shoving his brother's shoulder with his hand.

"We said no football talk," Callie's mum said.

"You said no work talk," Ryan replied. He winked at Mac.

Callie's mum rolled her eyes. She looked so much like Callie when she did that, it was scary. "I'm going to check on the caterers, and get you glasses for your beer. You're not drinking from bottles when the guests arrive."

Caterers? Beer in glasses? Mac thought. Bloody hell this party was already getting out of hand.

"Can you tell she hates football?" Mark asked.

"Loathes it," Ryan agreed.

"It's why we talk about it every chance we get," Anthony said with a grin. Mac realised that although

Callie got her looks from her mother, their personalities couldn't be more different. Thank goodness she seemed to get that from her father. This meet the parents things might not go so badly after all, as long as she avoided Callie's mum.

"And now Collette's not here, we can talk business," Ryan said, clapping Mac on the back. "Come on. We'll go outside where party poopers can't hear us."

"Is that code for grilling the new daughter-in-law about her intentions?" Mac asked as she followed Ryan back outside to the terrace.

Anthony chuckled. "Dad actually means he wants to talk business."

"Oh." Mac took a long drink of her beer. She had a feeling she'd be doing more listening than talking, but if this was what it took to impress Callie and prove that she could be part of her family, then she'd suck it up and do it.

"Callie tells us you've got a small greengrocer shop in Brisbane," Ryan said. "How's that doing?"

"Oh, er, it's okay, I guess."

"Any thoughts on expanding?"

"Expanding?"

"Franchising, or opening more stores? Callie said you've branched out into a couple of value-added product lines."

Mac had to think quickly. What would he mean by value-added product lines? Before she could say anything, Anthony said, "The one thing the big boys do well is all that extra stuff that taps into that convenience market. Recipe cards with pre-cut vegetables, pre-made meals. It's a whole new market."

Mac let out a breath. Now she knew what they were talking about. "Oh, yes, our fruit and antipasto platters sell like crazy, especially leading up to Christmas."

Ryan nodded approvingly. "What sort of margin are you getting?"

"Dad, Mac doesn't want to tell you all her secrets. I'm sure she's perfectly capable of running her own business."

My own business? What on earth had Callie been telling them?

"I think you've got the wrong end of the stick," Mac said.

"How do you mean?" Ryan asked.

"I don't own the shop, I'm the manager."

Ryan looked confused for a moment before he shook his head and smiled. "Right. I thought Callie said it was your business, but I might have misheard."

"She probably said you ran it," Anthony offered.

Mac smiled and nodded. "Well, that's not far from the truth." She took a sip of her beer. Had Callie lied to her father about what Mac did? Mac shook herself. Callie didn't lie. She hated lying.

"So, Callie said you run a party planning business," Mac said, trying to take the focus off of her. "Is that why you've planned this fancy party?"

Mark smiled into his beer and Mac got the distinct feeling that she'd said something stupid.

"It is, actually," Ryan said. "We mainly do corporate events at Rynotech now, but we've called in a few favours for the party tonight. Only the best for our girl."

There was an awkward silence, and Anthony broke it, thankfully, when he asked, "Let's go get refills." He nodded toward the house. "You can come and see Dad's beer collection."

"He has a beer collection? Isn't it supposed to be wine?" Mac asked as she followed Anthony across the patio.

"Dad didn't grow up in money," Anthony explained as he opened a door and ushered Mac inside. He lowered his voice. "He hates all the pretence and networking he has to do for the business."

"Really?"

Anthony pulled open another door and stepped aside for Mac to enter. "That's where Mum comes in handy. She loves that stuff."

"Would never have guessed," Mac said, making Anthony laugh. She stepped into the room. Her jaw dropped as she took it all in. It was decked out like you'd expect a wine cellar, only it was chilled like a cold room and full from ceiling to floor of different sorts of beer. Callie's Dad had his very own bottle shop right inside his house.

"Take your pick," Anthony said, spreading his hands wide.

Mac ran her hands across the shelving, picking up a bottle every now and then to read the label and then putting it back. Was it possible to have too much choice?

"I can't believe you got down here on trucks," Anthony said. He picked up a bottle and handed it to Mac. "It's impressive. Here, try this one."

"Yeah, well, I hope Callie's impressed," Mac replied, reading the label on the beer Anthony had given her. She still couldn't believe Callie never told her how much money her family actually had. It made Mac even more nervous. Callie could walk away from Mac and into the arms of some rich woman, which is probably exactly what her parents wished she'd do, judging by the way Mrs Preston had acted earlier. "Cantillon Gwerze?"

"Close," Anthony said. "Cantiyon Gooze. The Champagne of Belgium."

"Where does your dad get all of this stuff?" Mac asked.

"Dad's got a beer sommelier," Anthony explained. He took the bottle of *Cantillon Gueuze* from Mac, popped off the top and poured it into two glasses. He stuck his nose in the glass, like he was taste testing a wine and then took a sip.

Mac did the same and squeezed her eyes shut. "Totally not what I was expecting," she said. It tasted nothing like a beer she'd ever tasted. It was a little bit fruity, and a little bit sour, but it was definitely beer.

"It's... not bad. I'm not sure I could drink a six-pack of these, but one or two would be okay."

"This one's three hundred dollars a bottle," Anthony said. "So yes, a six-pack would probably be out of the question."

Mac coughed down her next gulp of beer, making Anthony laugh. "Won't your dad be upset we're drinking it?"

"He's got a couple more," Anthony said. "He'll be fine."

Mac had another drink of her expensive beer. No point wasting it, now that it was open.

"Callie loves you, you know," Anthony said.

"Did," Mac replied. "She didn't even tell you we'd broken up until this morning."

Anthony picked up the bottle and motioned to Mac to pick up another glass and walked to the cellar door. "Dad will want to have a drink now we've opened it," he explained. He closed the door behind them. "Why do you think she never told us?"

"She was embarrassed, probably," Mac replied.

Anthony smiled and shook his head. "I think she might be regretting it."

Mac stopped near the back door and turned. "You think so?"

Anthony nodded. "She tells me everything, normally. I mean, I knew before you did that your parents were surprising you a few weeks ago."

That was news to Mac. "Did you?"

"Callie busts herself with excitement over stuff like that. She needed to tell someone otherwise she would've spilled the beans to you."

Mac thought on that for a moment. "So, she never told you we'd broken up?"

"Nope. Never even mentioned you'd had a fight until this morning."

None of what Anthony said made any sense.

"So, you only found out today?"

Anthony nodded. "Picking Callie up from the airport by herself was a pretty big giveaway that something was up."

Mac was trying to process this latest information when Callie came bursting through the door from the kitchen, pushed past them and slamming the door behind her as she stormed outside.

"Well, that didn't take long," Anthony said with a sigh.

"What didn't take long?" Mac asked.

"Mum and Cal butt heads, they always have," Anthony replied.

Mac handed Anthony the empty glass. "I think I should go and see if she's okay."

Chapter 24

Mac reached the guest house just in time to see Callie slamming the door behind her. Mac opened the door and called, "Callie? Are you okay?"

"Go away, Mac," came a muffled reply.

Mac placed her beer glass on the kitchen bench and, following the sound of Callie's voice, found her star-fished on her stomach on the bed, a pillow pulled over her head. Mac sat down on the foot of the bed, resisting the urge to pat Callie's leg. "Is everything okay?"

Callie mumbled a reply that Mac couldn't understand.

"Is there something I can do?" Mac tried.

Callie lifted her head. She'd obviously been crying. "You've done enough, don't you think?"

"Me? What did I do?"

Callie rolled her eyes and dropped her head back onto the bed. "Why did you even come here, Mac?"

"What, right now? Or in general?"

Callie sighed into her pillow and rolled over and sat up, pulling her knees into her chest. "This isn't funny, Mac."

"Who's joking?"

"If you'd just stayed in Brisbane, none of this would've happened."

"I chased after you, Callie. I thought that's what you wanted."

Callie snorted. "Well, you thought wrong."

"And anyway," Mac said. "If you'd told your family we'd broken up, they wouldn't be throwing us this stupid party."

"We haven't broken up, Mac."

"Haven't we?" Mac asked. "I thought—"

"You thought me walking out after our argument was us breaking up?"

"But you took your clothes. And your toothbrush. You didn't answer any of my calls or texts. What was I supposed to think?"

"You were supposed to feel bad," Callie replied. "Just like I did."

Mac stood up and paced across the floor. "You ignored me because you wanted me to feel bad?"

Callie stood up too and glared across the room. "Yes, I did. You made me feel like crap, Mac, the way you lied."

"You lied too," Mac retorted.

Callie snorted. "Me? How did I lie?"

Mac blinked. "You told your parents I owned Stanley's shop."

Callie shrunk back and looked at the ground. When she didn't answer, Mac said, "Why would you do that, Callie? Are you ashamed of me?"

Callie shook her head.

"Is that the type of person you want to marry?" Mac pushed. "Someone who has money? Someone who has their own business?"

"No!" Callie cried. "That's not why I did it." She let out a sob and wiped her hand across her nose. "I just... I just wanted them to accept you."

"Accept me?"

Callie nodded and when she looked up, Mac could see the pain and sadness in her eyes. "You don't know what she's like. Mum's... My family are nothing like your family."

"I don't think there is anyone like my family," Mac replied. She gave a half-smile but got nothing in return from Callie. "It seems like we might be even, then," Mac said.

"This isn't a competition," Callie said. "And anyway, it doesn't change the fact that you asked me to marry you when you had no intention of actually doing it."

"No, I didn't," Mac said.

"Yes, you did," Callie replied.

Mac crossed her arms. "I never actually asked you to marry me."

"Oh, so I just imagined it then?" Callie asked.

"Think about it," Mac replied. "Think about that morning and what I actually said."

Callie looked around the room, apparently trying to remember two weekends ago. "You gave me the present, and I— oh."

Mac was about to say I told you so when Anthony barged in.

"Sorry, I didn't mean to interrupt but, Mac, someone called Kate has been calling on Callie's phone. It sounds important."

"What are you doing with my phone?" Callie asked.

"You left it in the kitchen," Anthony shrugged.

Mac took the phone. "Kate?"

"Mac! I've been calling and calling—"

"Slow down. Is everything okay?"

Kate paused and let out a breath. "It's Leila. She's had a heart attack."

Chapter 25

When they got to Leila's hospital room, Callie pulled Mac aside. "I'll go and see what I can find out. I'll be back in a minute."

Mac nodded. She took a deep breath, knocked on the open door and stepped in. Sophie rushed over and Mac wrapped her in a hug.

"How is she?" Mac asked.

Sophie stepped back. "She's okay. They've given her something to help her sleep. I don't know. We're waiting on tests."

Mac squeezed Sophie's hand. "Callie's gone off to pull the nurse thing and make sure they're doing the right stuff."

Sophie nodded and smiled tiredly. "We didn't even know she had a heart condition."

"She didn't tell you?" Max asked.

Sophie shook her head.

"She probably didn't want to worry you," Mac said. "Where's your dad?"

"Downstairs getting some coffee. Did you want any? I can call him and—"

"It's okay, Soph. I can go and get something later. How are you doing?"

Sophie shrugged and chewed on her lip. "We nearly lost her, Mac." She squeezed her eyes shut.

Mac pulled her into another hug and let her sob into her shoulder. "She'll be okay," Mac soothed her.

Sophie sniffled and pulled away and they both stood looking down at Leila lying asleep in the bed. She was normally so boisterous and full of life, it was jarring seeing her looking so fragile.

There was a knock at the door, and they both turned to see Callie walk in. "This is one of the best hospitals, Soph," Callie said. "She's in good hands."

"Thanks," Sophie nodded.

"Kate shouldn't be too far away," Mac said. "You know they had to fly first class to get here."

Sophie nodded. "I told her not to come, but she insisted. The plane tickets must have cost them a fortune."

"Andy's loaded. He can afford it," Mac shrugged.

When Callie dug her in the ribs and glared at her, Mac said, "I didn't say it was a bad thing. I meant that it's just as well he has money to be able to get Kate here so quickly, that's all."

"I still can't believe Kate has a boyfriend," Sophie said.

"I know," Mac replied. "It's weird, isn't it?"

Sophie smiled. "A little."

Sophie's dad returned with coffee. "Oh, sorry, guys. I didn't know you'd be here. I can go back down and get you something."

"That's okay. We should go get something to eat anyway," Callie said. She cocked her head towards the door and Mac took the hint.

"Yeah. I'm starving. I haven't had anything to eat since this morning," she said and followed Callie out of the room.

❧

"What football team should I be barracking for?" Mac asked as they ate in the hospital cafe.

Callie pulled the crusts off her sandwich. "What?"

"Your dad and brothers want to know which football team I barrack for, and since I have no idea about AFL or barracking, I don't want to say the wrong team and have them kick me out of the house."

Callie snorted. "Just don't say Collingwood."

"Not Collingwood. Got it." Mac took a bite of her sandwich, chewed and swallowed. "Which football team do you barrack for?"

"Collingwood," Callie replied.

"Oh," Mac said. "Is that a rebellion thing?"

Callie didn't answer. Instead she asked, "Why are you so interested in football for all-of-a-sudden?"

Mac shrugged. She'd been thinking about what Callie had said earlier, about their families being so different, and she'd realised that for everything she knew about her, Callie had never really mentioned her childhood, or her family, much at all.

"You've never talked about growing up," Mac said.

"It was nothing special," Callie said.

"Growing up in that house was nothing special?" Mac said, her eyebrows raised. "That house is pretty special. I would've killed to live in a house like that when I was a kid."

"Well," Callie said. "It was probably nothing like you imagined."

"So, no petting zoos for birthday parties or people making you snacks when you wanted them or cleaning up after you and making your bed?" Mac said. "Because that's what I imagined growing up in a house like that must have been like when I was a kid."

"Oh, we had all of that," Callie said. "But the one thing you wouldn't have imagined was having an overbearing mother like mine."

"Is that why you don't get along now?"

"It's just..." Callie stopped, sucked in a breath and let it out. "My mother had big expectations for me. I was supposed to become a doctor or a lawyer."

"You became a nurse, though," Mac said. "I think that's pretty great."

Callie smiled. "You're biased."

"Maybe, but I still count, don't I?"

Callie didn't answer. She picked up Mac's discarded piece of tomato, placed it on her own sandwich and took a bite. "A nurse isn't good enough for my mother."

"Why not? You're always telling me how it's nurses who have the hardest jobs."

"Having a nurse in the family isn't as prestigious as a doctor in the family."

"Why didn't Anthony become a doctor? Or Mark?"

Callie scoffed. "Anthony hates blood and Mark would never have made it through medical school. He hates studying."

"So why isn't your mum disappointed in them?"

"Oh, she is," Callie said. "They ignore her and make fun of it."

Mac could see that, the way they had teased their mother earlier. She was uptight, that was for sure, but surely she had some good qualities?

"But you can't."

Callie shook her head. "Mum and I just clash. We always have. I mean, she just doesn't listen to anything I want." Callie's voice rose, just a little. "The stupid engagement party is a perfect example. You know I almost told her the truth about us, just so she'd have to cancel it and ring all her friends and explain to them why the party was off."

"Why didn't you?" Mac asked.

Callie was quiet for a long time. "I don't know."

Mac felt like this could be her opening. Her one chance to say what she needed to say and hope that Callie still loved her. *Don't stuff it up.*

Mac took a deep breath. "Callie, I'm so sorry for how things have turned out."

"Mac—"

"Please just let me say this, Callie. I've been avoiding it for so long but I need you to hear this stuff." She paused, hoping Callie would let her continue.

"Okay," Callie said.

Mac continued. "That day, with Mum and Dad, was never meant to happen like that. When Mum and Dad turned up, I was just...thrown off. And then Mum was hassling me about not losing you because of my commitment issues."

The corners of Callie's lips twitched up.

"Yes, I know I have issues, but I was going to make a commitment that day. Just not a marriage one." Mac pulled a jewellery box out of her pocket. When Callie's eyes opened wider, Mac reassured her. "It's not a ring. That's in my bag back at your parents' place."

"Oh."

Mac pushed the box across the table. "This is the present you were supposed to get. I was going to ask you to move in with me."

Callie flipped open the lid and inside was a heart-shaped keyring, split in two, and engraved with their initials. Callie stared down at the box, not saying anything.

"This is the present I was supposed to get?" she asked, finally.

Mac nodded.

Callie's face broke into a smile and then she put her hand to her mouth and giggled.

"What's so funny?" Mac asked.

"Can you imagine poor Mr Mackenzie getting this instead of his ring, and popping the question and presenting his girlfriend with this?"

Mac laughed and shook her head. "Poor bloke."

Callie snorted. "Poor girlfriend." She pulled the keyrings out of the box and turned them over in her hand. "Were you really going to ask me to move in with you?"

"I was." Mac swallowed hard. "I still am."

Mac tried to read Callie's expression, but she wasn't giving anything away. For a moment, Mac thought she'd missed her chance, and then Callie placed the remainder of her sandwich on her plate and looked up.

She nodded.

"You will?" Mac asked.

"Yes. I'll move in with you," Callie said. She leaned forward and kissed Mac on the lips. She tasted like ham and cheese with a hint of tomato.

"Mac!" Kate's voice broke through their blissful moment.

Mac jumped up and gave Kate a hug. When Kate pulled back, she said, "Looks like you two are okay?"

Mac nodded. "Callie's moving in."

Kate gasped and looked from Mac to Callie. "Really?"

Callie nodded.

"Congratulations!" Kate said, pulling Mac into another hug. She whispered in Mac's ear, "Looks like the road trip worked."

"I never want to do that again." She pulled away and looked past Kate. "Where's Andy?"

"At the motel," Kate replied. "He didn't want to intrude, so he'll come up later. How's Leila?"

"She was sleeping when we got here, but she was okay, I think."

"They're waiting on some more tests," Callie said.

"Should we go up?" Kate asked.

Mac nodded.

As they walked to the elevators, Kate said, "Poor Leila. All she wanted was a white Christmas."

"Maybe they can go again next year," Mac said. "Maybe we can all go and have a white Christmas next year."

Callie squeezed Mac's hand. "You know what? I think I might get going."

"Are you sure?" Mac asked.

Callie nodded. "You should spend some time with your friends. Call me later and I'll come and pick you up." She kissed Mac on the cheek and hugged Kate.

Mac watched her leave and Kate said, "I'm so glad you worked things out."

Mac grinned. "Me too."

"No engagement, though," Kate teased.

The elevator arrived and she stepped in. Mac stepped in after her.

"Give me time," Mac replied.

Chapter 26

Sophie, Mac and Kate lay on the lounge chairs in the waiting room, watching a replay of the Christmas carols on television.

"Pity you didn't get to see that live," Kate said. "It's pretty amazing."

"Callie hates Christmas carols," Mac replied. She was just barely keeping her eyes open. She'd had a huge last two days and it was finally catching up on her.

"Does she?" Sophie asked.

Mac shrugged. "Yep. Weird, huh?" She watched as the final song was sung and the credits started to roll. The screen went black and the name of a company popped up on screen that Mac thought sounded familiar. She sat up in her chair and thought hard where she'd heard the name Rynotech Events.

"Holy crap!" she said.

"What?" Kate asked, startled.

"That's Callie's family's business."

"What is?" Sophie asked.

"The company that put on the carols."

Sophie looked at Mac, confused. "Are you sure?"

Mac nodded and pulled out her phone. She googled Rynotech Events and sure enough, there they were, the events company listed as the organiser of the Melbourne Christmas carols.

Mac cringed. "Oh, God."

"What's wrong?" Kate asked.

"I called them party planners," Mac said. When Sophie and Kate laughed, Mac said, "You've got no idea how embarrassing that is."

Sophie's dad appeared in the doorway. "You have to come and see this," he said and then turned and hurried off.

Kate, Mac and Sophie followed him down the hall to the windows at the end and looked out. There was some sort of fair in the park across the road.

"Is that—?" Kate started.

"—snow?" Sophie finished.

"Holy crap," Mac said. Her phone buzzed in her pocket. It was a message from Callie. *Can you see the snow machine?* Mac scanned the park until she saw the snow machine off to the side. She text back *I see it.*

Callie sent back *That's me waving.*

Mac looked again and sure enough, there was Callie, waving like mad. "There's Callie," Mac said.

"Where?" Kate asked.

Mac pointed her out and Kate and Sophie waved back madly. "What's she doing down there?" Sophie asked.

"I have no idea," Mac replied. "But I guess I should go down and find out."

❧

"You did this?" Mac asked.

Callie nodded.

"How?"

"I called in some favours," Callie replied, nodding over to where a jumping castle was being set up. Anthony waved at them and Mac waved back, dumbfounded.

"It's what we do," Callie said.

"Is that your family slogan?" Mac asked. "Because I've heard that so many times today."

Callie laughed. "It is, actually."

Mac looked around at the snow machines and the jumping castle and the giant candy canes and snow men and the food vans, amazed that Callie could get it all organised at such short notice. "Why did you do all this?"

Callie shrugged. "We couldn't let Leila and Sophie and her dad miss out on a white Christmas."

Mac shook her head. "You're amazing, you know that?"

"I know," Callie said, grinning. "Want to see what else we organised?"

"Sure," Mac said, as she linked arms with Callie and let her lead the way into the park.

They bought ice-creams and sat on a park bench, watching as kids filtered down from the hospital to catch fake snow and get selfies with Santa.

Mac looked at Callie and realised that she'd come so close to stuffing things up, and she didn't want to do that again. She didn't want to risk losing Callie ever again.

Callie saw Mac looking at her. "What?"

A whole lot of words and feelings and memories went whizzing around Mac's head. If ever there was a time to propose, now would be it. She took a deep breath and took hold of Callie's hand. "I love you, Callie. A whole lot, actually, and I never, ever, in my wildest dreams thought I'd find someone like you. I mean, you can ask Kate and Sophie. They were sure I'd end up by myself too."

"Mac—"

"When I was in hospital and I thought I was dying—"

"It was a panic attack," Callie cut in.

Mac put up her hand. "I thought I was dying, Cal, but you were there, and you made me feel safe. And then Kate came in and told me I'd be totally stupid to let you go."

"Did she?"

Mac nodded. "She did, and I agree with her. And I know you think I can be stupid sometimes, but I'm definitely not stupid enough to let you go without asking you to—"

"Mac—"

Mac finally stopped and took a breath. Her heart was beating a million miles an hour. This was it. Even though Callie had agreed to move in with her, Mac knew that wasn't enough. She wanted to be with Callie, and she was pretty sure Callie wanted to be with her. "I don't care if your mum hates me."

"She doesn't—"

"I don't care if they don't think I'm good enough for you."

"Mac—"

"Marry me, Callie."

Mac locked eyes with Callie, and she felt like time had stopped, waiting for Callie to answer.

"Are you sure, Mac?" Callie asked.

Mac nodded.

"Because I don't want you to be asking me in a desperate attempt to make me want to stay, because I've already told you that I don't want to break up with you."

"I know," Mac said.

"And I already said I'd move in with you, and that's a huge thing for you already," Callie said.

Mac nodded. "I know, and I'm sure. I want to marry you, Callie. I'm sorry it took me so long to get my shit together."

Callie's face softened and she squeezed Mac's hand. "Yes," she said.

"Yes?" Mac asked, not quite sure she heard right.

Callie nodded. "Yes, Mac, I'll marry you."

Mac took Callie's face in her hands and kissed her. When she sat back, she said, "Are we going to have to let your parents organise the wedding?"

Callie laughed. "I think you know the answer to that."

Mac put her arm around Callie's shoulder and hugged her close. "Probably better than my family organising it." Then she had a horrible thought. "They're going to have to meet each other now, aren't they?"

Callie snuggled in closer. "Don't destroy the moment, Mac."

Mac kissed the top of Callie's head and watched as Kate and Andy, and Sophie, Leila and Sophie's dad wandered around the fake snow-covered park and realised that, even though the circumstances weren't great, they'd all get to spend Christmas together after all.

The End

A Note from SR

I hope you enjoyed reading Dashing All the Way as much as I enjoyed writing it. This one has been a long time coming. I started it back in 2017 and it's taken me that long to come up with an ending I was happy with. It's a sequel, of sorts, to my Christmas novella, Three Wishes, though you don't need to have read it to read this one. (If you haven't read it yet, you should!)

The story is inspired by all of my favourite Christmas movies - the ones where accidents happen, and family turn up unannounced and the characters try to get through the holidays unscathed. The ones where family can simultaneously be the most annoying and loving people at the same time.

If you have a few minutes, I'd love an honest review on the site you bought Dashing All the Way from. Reviews help readers find books they love and encourage new readers to take a chance on authors they might not have tried before. Even a short note on what you thought about the books you read makes a huge difference, and of course, each and every review I get means a lot to me, so thank you so much if you write one!

If you want to get in touch with me directly, you can do that via email or social media. I love hearing from readers and answer every message and email I get. I am most active on Twitter and Facebook, and can be found posting pictures of my dogs, coffee and home brew beer on Instagram.

Email - selena@srsilcox.com
Facebook - srsilcox
Instagram - @srsilcox
Twitter - @srsilcox

And if you want to know when the next book is ready, be sure to sign up to my email list, which you can do at https://bit.ly/33OhUgQ

Thanks for reading, and Merry Christmas!

Acknowledgements

A huge thank-you to Michael Wait, who helped me with the logistics of getting Mac from Brisbane to Melbourne via courier truck. To KJ, JL Heylen and Jane Waterton (all awesome Aussie lesfic authors) for your fantastic advice on the first draft. Your insights into the AFL and Toorak made the story that much richer.

To my Beta Readers, Elisabeth, Randi, and Amy, thanks for your comments, advice, and feedback, and for picking up the typos and errant full stops. It's amazing how many of those I miss after I've read the story so many times...

To Alison Bedford, who for some reason keeps asking me to send her more of my stuff, and continues to make me learn more and get better with every new book, I hope I keep living up to your expectations with each new story. Thank you for making me a better writer over these past years and for all of your advice, counsel, enthusiasm and support.

To every reader who has taken my stories and characters to heart and loved them as much as I do, if not more, thank you too - you are the reason I keep writing.

Finally, to my wife, Teresa. You've waited a long time for this book (thank you for being so patient!) and thank you for believing in me when I don't. I love you a lot.

SR

xx

About the Author

S.R. Silcox started writing sweet romance stories for lesbian teens because she never got to read them when she was younger.

She quickly discovered it was a great way for her to relive her glory days from her childhood and make up for all the things she didn't do but wished she could have.

Like kiss cute girls and play professional cricket.

She currently writes sweet romances for lesbian tweens and teens, as well as the Alice Henderson series about girls who play cricket.

Amy's Rest is her first adult lesbian fiction novel.

She mostly hangs out on Twitter and Instagram, where she posts updates on her new house, sport, her dogs and trying to kick her procrastination habit.

She lives on the coast in (mostly) sunny Queensland, Australia with her wife and two dogs.

https://www.srsilcox.com
https://twitter.com/srsilcox
https://www.instagram.com/srsilcox
http://bit.ly/amysrestnews